CHICKENS THAT ARE NOT HER CHICKENS

Stories

By Mario E. Martinez

OTHER WORKS BY MARIO E. MARTINEZ

San Casimiro, Texas: Short Stories

Ashtree

A Pig Named Orrenius & Other Strange Tales

NEO-Laredo

Cipactli & The Glowing Pigs of El Cenizo

TABLE OF CONTENTS

"HE SINGS SONGS THAT MAKE MEN MAD. HANG HIM IN HIS JESTER'S GARB TO THE HIGHEST TOWER IN THE CITY. LET HIM MAKE RHYMES FOR THE VULTURES."

ROBERT E. HOWARD
"BY THIS AXE I RULE!"

"WHEN I WRITE SOMETHING I NEVER THINK ABOUT WHY."

CHARLES BUKOWSKI
Hollywood

THIN SOUP

I.

Isidro hoped no one noticed the soup was thin today but, in a remote factory hundreds of miles from any town, not a lot went unnoticed. The workers were tired, aching from days on the line, and there wasn't much around for recreation. The soup is what kept them going on the long shift. Fourteen hour stretches, six hour and fifty-five-minute shifts on either side of a ten-minute break. The soup kept the factory peaceful and not just on the floor or at the docks but in the barracks too.

If the soup was hearty like a chunky gravy, the factory would be a paradise of productivity. The workers smiled at one another when the long lines passed for a shift change. The men shook hands and wished one another luck like two little league teams at the end of a game. There was laughter. If the soup was chunky, no one even wanted to cheat at cards and that's how management liked it.

But the soup was thin that day. That was no surprise, though. The soup simmered all day and reduced a little faster after each ladle which was why buckets of water were poured into the pot after every lunch shift. Isidro had to do that a few times already and the workers could tell.

Isidro saw it in their eyes. They held their bowls like beggars' dishes and he poured them their soup.

The weight was the first clue. It got them looking into the bowl, then the wrinkled brows started. The looks of suspicion, of wanting to ask what kind of trick Isidro was pulling.

The looks would be all for a day or two before the snark came. But by the time management decided to look into it—and oh would they by the state of the soup—then snide remarks would be silly things to worry about in comparison.

II.

"It's a big pot and that means big responsibility," management had told Isidro and there was no lie to it. The soup pot was so huge—nearly ten feet from base to lip—that a platform and a series of stairs were made specifically to get to the top of it. The burner beneath it that kept the soup at a low simmer was nearly a foot tall itself.

It was a black iron relic of a bygone age and a few times Isidro heard rumors of its forging. The soup within, too, was mysterious and ancient, its beginnings unknown.

Who first made it, his mentor didn't know, nor did theirs, or the ones before. Isidro imagined some dusty relic had set water to boil with meats and vegetables and spices to serve one shift. The management of then, no doubt, told them to add a bucket of water instead of meats or greens until there were complaints. Some vegetable chunks and meat scraps would follow until, finally, the soup would need a real thickening. That's when Isidro's assistant, Azalea, would be promoted and he... retired.

The day of the looks, Isidro asked Azalea to bring flour and corn starch because, as much as management wanted the soup adequate, the pantry was more regulated than the shipments. The powders thickened the soup enough that no one looked at Isidro funny, though a few grumbled to management that the soup was like paste in their mouths.

III.

Isidro felt management coming up the stairs before seeing him. Everyone called him management, but his name was Mitchell, a big old thing that waddled because of brittle knees and a big belly. Sometimes, people called him Big Tom, but never to his face.

He gave no "good morning" or so much as a "how are you." Instead, he got to the soup pot and looked in. After a moment, he presented an old teacup and waited wordlessly.

Isidro nodded and, with his big wooden ladle, mixed the soup around. Isidro could almost see through the morning's test pour so he hoped the stirring would make the soup appear thicker. Management got impatient and dipped the entire cup into the soup. He examined not just the soup pouring out of the cup but the bits that clung to the cup's interior.

Management divined the vegetable scraps and meat shreds before he brought the dripping cup to his mouth and touched the rim to his tongue. Smacking the flavor around his mouth, he eyed Isidro and spat the soup drippings onto the ground.

"The soup's thin," was all management said yet Isidro knew the handful of words were worse than any he'd ever heard.

The soup was thin and the factory didn't like thin soup because thin soup was like an omen. Thick soup was a sign of good, productive days with everyone glad to be shoulder to shoulder with their peers. But thin soup was a distraction. The workers stopped focusing on their jobs and cared less for one another. They started counting what they had and compared it to the next guy and the next until they compared themselves all the way to Big Tom's managerial door. Workers stole, workers lied, sometimes elbows bumped and before long the whole line was fighting and the conveyors had to be shut off.

Isidro thought as management stomped down the stairs. At the bottom of the stairs, management passed Azalea, who stood with her head bowed. When management was gone, she rushed to Isidro and asked what Big Tom had said.

Still looking at Big Tom's receding figure, Isidro replied, "Tonight, we need to check the traps."

"So soon?"

Isidro looked at her. The panic was clear in his wide, detached eyes. "The soup is thin," he told her and no more explanation was required.

IV.

Management and the cooks were the only ones who knew the truth about the traps. Sure, the workers saw them around, but they were used to not knowing things about the company. As it was, none of the workers really knew what the machines made, what the pieces were for, or even where they were sent. So, it was easy to ignore the traps–glue and snap and snare–which were tucked beneath every crate and pallet pile and dark corner of the factory. But three people knew the traps' double purpose.

Being the lone building for miles and miles, all kinds of vermin were attracted to the factory and its garbage. Racoons and rats which, in turn, brought out the snakes. The lights attracted bugs and the bugs then attracted bats. The traps were emptied into a chute that, to the rest of the factory's knowledge, led to an incinerator. In actuality, it led to a wash bin where the animals were skinned and butchered for the soup.

But it was springtime, so all the rodents found easier meals elsewhere and the bats were too clever to be caught by simple snares.

Still, Isidro and Azalea walked the factory and checked the traps during their own lunch. The two of them went through the factory floor as troops of men worked at gargantuan machines. Together, Isidro and Azalea crawled beneath the machinery and scuttled through the shadows in hopes of getting enough meat to keep the workers quiet.

At the end of the day, Isidro and Azalea met in the storeroom to inspect their harvest. Eight fat rats, a robin, and a toad.

"Maybe they'll do," Azalea offered.

Isidro sighed. "Sure. Maybe they'll buy me some time," he said, unable to sound convincing.

He butchered the vermin. Each time he stripped fur and organs, the meat shrank and shrank until the chunks hardly filled half a bucket. They were mixed with herbs, spices, and starches—anything to add mass. Even still, Azalea carried it up to the soup pot with barely a struggle and when she dumped in the meat, it hardly made a splash. The water Isidro had to add only made it worse. He tried to tell himself that everything needed time to thicken, to marry, to become one with the soup.

Isidro dreamed of the soup pot that night.

The cafeteria was dark and he was alone. The pot bubbled unseen but he heard it, smelled it, as he approached its song. Isidro's dream-self walked up the steps to the platform but once he reached it, he didn't want to look over the pot's rim. He already knew what was there. Faces. Dozens of faces, eyes vacant and mouths open in agony, rising out of the soup like potatoes.

One by one, the faces noticed Isidro, righted themselves, and beamed as if in recognition of an old friend.

Isidro woke when the final face turned to look at him. It was distorted by heat and wrinkles, but there was no mistaking that it was his own. It smiled and its dumb mouth formed words. "The soup is thin."

Isidro thought of his dream in the shower. There, he turned the hot water up to near-scalding and stood in it until he could endure it no longer.

V.

The first to complain was a wimp named Giovanni. Normally, Giovanni was a sheepish man of a hundred and eighty pounds who somehow fit into spaces much smaller than his frame. Often, he contorted himself between people in line or strafed the walls like they were mountain ledges to avoid even the appearance of rudeness. For him to scoff and say, "C'mon. This isn't soup. It's more like gruel," felt like justification for the others to join in.

"They skimping us *again*?" one voice asked from the line.

"Of-goddamn-course they are," someone responded from one of the long tables. "It's always the same. Just enough to keep us quiet but always–*fucking always*–skimping more and more."

"We're the ones doing all the work," another complained.

The agreement was deafening.

"Let's see what that fat ass Big Tom eats!" an old timer cried. "He eats real good for a man who just sits in his office collecting a good check."

"Why don't we drag him down here and see how much of this soup he can stand. We'll goddamn drown him in factory hospitality!"

Soon, pockets of people, narrow-eyed and sneering, stood, pounding the tables. From them came a dizzying medley of violent ideas, of the best ways to show management just what they thought. But before they could tear the long tables apart or raid toolboxes for weapons, the thin soup worked its disruptive spell.

Someone in the teeming mass tried snatching an unwatched bowl and half-a-dozen arms seized him, crying, "Cheat! Thief! Miserable cunt!" and a pathetic voice rang out, "He wasn't even eating it," which was true but not one of them cared.

The soup was thin and thin soup bore no brothers.

The workers pulled the thief in all directions, punching and gouging, as some took the hot soup and poured it on his head like anointing oils before using the empty bowls to knock dents in his skull and, in the tumult, more thieves were caught, tried, and judged by their coworkers who were now hardly more than hungry animals until the room was a chamber of body heat and blood-red justice.

Isidro watched in grim silence. He called Azalea to him and handed her his ladle. Without a word, Isidro untucked his shirt and unbuttoned the top button of it. Azalea stopped him.

"You don't have to," she begged. "They can last–"

He looked at his apprentice and sighed. He swept his hand over the mass of them. "The soup is thin."

He stripped completely. He handed his apron, shoes, shirt, pants, socks, and underwear to Azalea. Isidro took back his ladle and clanged the side of the pot until the reverberations drew everyone's attention.

Isidro walked to the edge of the platform and spoke in a calm, soothing tone. "It's all right, everyone," he said. "On behalf of management, the factory has heard you and agrees. The soup is thin. If you'll allow us a few minutes, I believe we'll have solved the issue to your satisfaction. Management appreciates your patience."

The workers, still half-beasts, attentively waited for Isidro.

He passed the ladle back to Azalea. "Remember what I told you," he said, taking the apron from her. "If it's floating, it's not cooking." He slipped the apron over her head and tied it.

Azalea held the ladle like a boatman's oar.

Isidro went to the soup pot and found the only face in it was a reflection of his own. He'd planned to climb over the rim and slide into the soup. He thought that'd be dignified. But, on contact with the iron pot, he yelped and fell over the rim, landing in the soup with a splash. Isidro thrashed, screaming and gasping for air in one confused instant, but Azalea forced him under the surface with the ladle.

The soup churned like an angry sea and Azalea almost felt like she heard Isidro's last words in the short-lived steam bubbling up from the soup. Eventually, the soup calmed.

"If everyone would please line up," Azalea called, her voice shaky. "Management believes the soup will be to your satisfaction."

–ETC.–

THE VOICE IN YOUR GUTS

I.

The voice was small at first and you really don't remember when it got so big. It used to be it would growl or whine like a dog. The voice would mirror your feelings and agree with your moods. It was even like a friend for a while. It would justify your anger, your sadness, and you'd say, "You're right about that," or whisper, "You know how it goes."

Somewhere along the way, though, in the summer between ninth grade and tenth, the voice in your guts got mean.

You've never been a pretty girl. Never skinny. When the voice in your guts first insulted you, you'd been at a family picnic in your father's hometown. It was summer and you wore a dress your mother bought at the mall. The dress flattered your figure and, though it wasn't your first choice, you thought it was nice looking.

Even your fashionable Tia Diana had told you how pretty you were. She was always well-dressed for her sales job at Riverside. She tip-toed over the grass to get to you, scooping up your plump cheeks and kissing them. "Que linda," she squealed. "That face!"

You remember thinking if you were born in a different century, your face would've been all that the boys saw. The rest of you would be a shameful secret covered by lace and heavy fabric.

At that moment, with your fat face in your tia's hands, you wanted to sink into the earth and die. A car filled with grimy small town high school kids drove by. You looked at them—their car was so noisy—and they whistled and catcalled in spanish. Your cheeks got red—sure, you thought they were idiots, but you didn't mind the attention. It was seldom anyone noticed you for your looks.

POOR SAD BITCH. YOU REALLY THINK THEY'RE LOOKING AT YOU?

You straightened up. The suddenness of the words, the masculine tone, they scared a cold sweat down your back. There wasn't any need to look around. Your tios and primos weren't nearby and none of them would've said anything like that to you anyway. The words, the cruelty and mockery, came from your guts. When you hugged yourself, it felt like something alien moved inside your belly.

SURE... THOSE HARD-ONS WANTED YOU, NOT HER, your guts told you, guiding you to look at your prima, Elvira.

Elvira was nineteen and dressed in little shorts and a littler shirt to show off her flat stomach and brown thighs. Her skin glowed and the wind made her hair sway seductively on her shoulders. Even with her sunglasses, her bored expression was evident. While you watched her, the voice in your guts laughed.

It was a quiet, deliberate laugh that told you it had all been some big joke. That laughter followed you until you sipped some warm soda to hide your watering eyes. For a second, you couldn't hear the voice anymore and, later that day, you ate so much the voice stayed quiet until you got home.

II.

You never gave the voice much chance to talk again. Whenever it came back, you ate to choke it.

The trick worked so well, you'd almost put the voice out of your mind until the day Federico walked down the hall at school and, despite that you usually kept your eyes on the floor, you stared at him. His smile was so carefree, so confident. You wanted to touch him as he passed, but you clutched your books tighter against your chest instead. Pulled by the sheer force of his personality, you followed him.

Once you'd completely turned around, the only people in front of you were Alexandra and her friends, Bonnie and Elena. Their faces shocked you and sweat beaded on the small of your back. To have their attention made you nervous. From birth to now, that trio had been fawned over and worshipped like they floated three feet above everyone else. They were thin and beautiful and had never wanted a thing to do with you.

Alexandra raised an eyebrow.

You felt like a girl condemned.

Her eyes went from you to Federico, who stopped to joke around with his teammates, and she gave you a vicious smile. "Freddy!" she sang.

Federico spotted her, smiled, and jogged over to Alexandra. She kissed him hard, lingering on his lips while her friends smirked at you. Alexandra told him she'd see him later and he left for class.

He didn't look at you once.

Alexandra seemed to enjoy your pained expression. She pouted and gave you a drawn-out *awww*. "Oh, you like him? I could set you two up, but... I think he likes girls, not cows. I could still ask though. If you really want me to."

You started to cry a stony, silent stream of tears.

"Did you really think Freddy would ever—*ever*!—want to see all your rolls and stretch marks or your flabby pig-cunt?" Alexandra had said, almost hissing the last word, before she and her friends went to class.

You closed your eyes against the stares of passing people. Their acknowledgements left a slimy residue. And, as you'd gulped down your tears, you heard it again.

WHAT ARE YOU CRYING FOR? the voice in your guts asked. *YOU ALREADY KNEW YOU HAD ROLLS AND STRETCH MARKS AND A FLABBY PIG-CUNT, RIGHT, YOU POOR SAD BITCH? I FEEL YOU MESSING WITH IT WHEN EVERYONE'S ASLEEP.*

The voice wouldn't get quiet until after lunchtime.

III.

It got to where you knew two things about the voice. The first was it got louder every day. It was in your dreams and, during your waking hours, it wouldn't stop. It didn't matter what mood you were in either. Not anymore. The voice in your guts was a cruel narrator, telling you things like the friction of your thighs rubbing together was the only warmth your vagina would get or, if a teacher asked a question you knew the answer to, it would say, *SPARE US THE OINKS, WILL YOU? LIKE A DUMB PIG-BITCH LIKE YOU KNOWS ANYTHING.* That near-constant commentary led you to the next truth about the voice in your guts.

Whenever you ate, the voice went silent. The heavier the meal, the longer the quiet.

You carried those secrets all through school. You hid cupcakes and cookies and brownies, anything, to shut the voice up so you could concentrate enough to graduate. Once you got your diploma, a part of you hoped the voice would go away on its own. The snooty girls and perverted guys were probably what triggered it, you'd reasoned before it laughed at you once again.

The voice in your guts followed you to college in the northeast. Eating so much was expensive, but anything was better than having to listen to it.

The eating and resulting silence got to be a sort of ritual. In the morning, you ate heavy breakfasts and snacked until lunch, which, usually, never kept the voice quiet until dinner. Part of why you went to a school so far away from Texas was that no one would care about your hermetic lifestyle.

The blizzard stopped that.

Most of the other students were gone for winter break and, unlike other floors where a few stragglers remained, your floor was empty. The solitude was refreshing. You went about your food rituals without worrying about any judging eyes. You ate take-out, paid over the phone, and pretended not to speak english when the delivery guy commented about the storm.

When the snows came, at first, the only problem was the food came slower which meant the voice rumbled more and more between meals—those spaces got more frequent the more the snows fell.

The snow didn't stop the next day or the next. The city was under a blanket seven feet deep and the only option was to wait it out. No stores were open, no places delivered, all was quiet.

Except the voice.

The food ran out quick. The fear that an unfinished meal might have the voice going again prompted you to gorge. You even braved a walk to the vending machine at the end of the hall, but all it had was gum. You decided to go to the one downstairs and told yourself a meal of corn chips and packaged cookies was a better offering to the voice than nothing.

Yet, once your hand settled on the stairwell door, the voice in your guts laughed.

THEY'LL LOVE THAT, WON'T THEY? it said. *THE FAT TROG WADDLING OUT OF HER CAVE. AND WHERE DOES SHE GO? RIGHT TO THE FUCKING SNACKS! OH, YOU'RE A PIG, ALL RIGHT. A PREDICTABLE LITTLE PIG.*

You pushed the door open and started downstairs. The voice giggled at each step. It pointed out every bounce and ripple of your flesh.

By the time you got to the next floor, you were humming just to distract yourself from the voice asking if you intended to eat the whole dorm into starvation. You got to the vending machine and pumped your handful of coins into the slot. When you thought it was enough, you pressed buttons at random. You didn't care what came out only that it would make the voice be quiet.

You realized too late that the machine ate your money. In a panic, you banged on the sides of the vending machine and shook it on its legs.

OH YEAH. LET'S GET ALL THESE PEOPLE OUT HERE. LET THEM LOOK AT THE PIG CRYING AT AN EMP-TY TROUGH, the voice teased.

You shook your head, thinking you'd just go down another floor. There had to be a working machine somewhere. But, when you looked in your hand, there were only nickels and pennies there. Frantic, you looked at the hall behind you. Your eyes went to the bottoms of doors in hopes of seeing slits of light—any evidence of people.

HAVE SOME SHAME, YOU GROSS BITCH. YOU SLOB, the voice told you. *YOU REALLY WANT TO GO KNOCKING ON DOORS, BEGGING FOR CHANGE SO YOU CAN STUFF YOUR FAT-FUCK FACE? WHAT A DAY TO BE ALIVE. C'MON PIGGY PIG-PIG. GO. GIVE ALL THESE LONELY SHITS A REASON TO CALL HOME.*

The tears found you.

FUCK, IF YOU'RE GOING TO BLUBBER LIKE THAT, GO TO YOUR ROOM, the voice demanded in disgust. *AT LEAST ALL THESE COCKSUCKERS WON'T THINK YOU'RE HEARTBROKEN OVER NOT GETTING YOUR CANDY.*

"Please... just go away," you whispered.

THEN LET ME GO, YOU POOR SAD BITCH, the voice said, laughing. *NOT EVEN I WOULD BE AROUND YOU IF I HAD THE CHOICE.*

IV.

Back at your dorm room, there was half a box of stale cereal and a canned fruit cocktail. Before the tv went out, the news reported the blizzard wouldn't let up for days. You told yourself you'd have to ration the little food you had—the voice thought the plan was hilarious—but you ended up eating most of your food in one sitting. You hoped it might make the voice stop.

But the food barely calmed it for an hour or two.

The voice returned with the hunger pangs. *DID YOU HONESTLY THINK YOU HAD SELF-CONTROL? LOOK AT YOURSELF. ALMOST THREE HUNDRED POUNDS, STRETCH PANTS TOO TIGHT AND YOUR BIG SHIRT CAN BARELY CONTAIN YOUR TITS. WHO'S THAT FOOLING? YOU'RE A BREATHING GARBAGE DISPOSAL. A TUBE FROM MOUTH TO ASSHOLE WITH LEGS. YOU'RE JUST A FAT, BORING VIRGIN WHO CAN'T REMEMBER WHEN SHE COULD SEE HER OWN MUFF.*

The voice didn't relent.

It was your lullaby. You woke to its laughter and a wooden emptiness in your stomach. The voice wondered aloud at how much your parents probably wished for a daughter that wouldn't have to settle for whatever limp-dick could stand her sweat-sour pussy long enough to impregnate her.

That day, you laid there in bed and let the voice in your

guts go over every shame and humiliation until you couldn't cry another tear.

LOOK ON THE BRIGHT SIDE. A LITTLE DEHYDRA-TION'LL BE GOOD FOR YOUR WAISTLINE, the voice chided.

You weren't sure how long the voice went on, but it cackled when you clutched your cramping stomach. The voice speculated how long it would take for you to be reduced to chewing on belts and shoe leather. But you noticed something, a small positive. The voice, it seemed, was getting tired.

Though it still attacked, the energy and venom coming from your guts had weakened. By nightfall, you were woozy and lightheaded, but the voice couldn't manage words and had to settle for mocking snorts and scoffs as your starved mind wandered over thoughts of food.

These moments of silence gave you little joy but gave you peace enough to sleep and to dream.

V.

You dreamed you were naked in the snow. The city was silent and white. The windows were dark, frozen over with thin layers of ice. In the dream, you were not ashamed of your nudity. You looked down at your body like it was alien, your bulging belly the most fascinating part. When you put your hands to it, your fingers entered the flesh like it was mud. Soon, you were up to your forearms in soft skin. Your fingers felt your slimy guts and, amidst the soft squish of your innards, you felt something hard, rigid, like a jagged stone. You took it in your hands and pulled. It resisted against the dreamy slickness of your guts but, eventually, came out clean. In your bloody hands, you held a rough-hewn idol with a face as inhuman as it was cruel. You held it up and saw it fret in its slumber like a living infant on the verge of screaming itself awake.

Its horrible eyes opened and examined you and it called to you with its terrible voice.

VI.

Awake, your hands went to your belly, probing it until the voice sighed. *IT'S ALL STILL THERE,* it told you. When you didn't relent, you felt it groan. *IT'S SIX INCHES SOUTH. HIT THE ASSHOLE AND YOU WENT TOO FAR.*

You were both starving and it said no more after that.

Its silence shocked you.

Slowly, thoughts rolled in. You wondered if the voice maybe wasn't like a baby, perpetually hungry and easily agitated. It raged until you ate, feeding it and silencing it until the next tantrum. But like with all living things, the fight didn't last once the sustenance was gone. The voice in your guts might want to claw and scream, but, sooner or later, it wouldn't have the stamina for it.

You waited a few minutes for the voice to say something, but all you got was silence and the feeling your thoughts were being observed.

You squeezed your flab and smiled, thinking all you had to do was starve the voice. You could outlast it. You had the reserves, you thought, to its amusement.

VII.

The idea the voice was something separate like a parasite gave you relief rather than dread. For all those years of torment, you thought it was just the inner tyrant, that other-self forged and implanted by the world, and all the horrible things it said were just the truths you held in your heart.

But, if it was something removed from you, perhaps you weren't just A WORTHLESS BITCH as the voice often called you, but the victim of some cruel cosmic mistake, chosen at random to endure the constant vitriol living within you.

For the next two days, you drank only water and even then only enough to survive since each sip gave the voice a little life. Its tone was so weak, the insults bolstered your resolve instead of harmed it.

The lack of food didn't leave you unscathed. You were weak and dizzy, too exhausted to move far from bed. Your stomach acids sloshed like trapped stretches of angry ocean. The prolonged hunger didn't color your thoughts so much as all the tiny humiliations were repainted by your revelation about the voice.

The snacks in bed or the tearful gorge-fests before your parents got home from work. At one point, not long ago, these moments filled you with profound guilt. Now, you were the tragic hero desperate to survive. When your pants split junior year or when you got the nerve to ask a boy to dance only to have him and his friends laugh in your face. None of those moments were your fault. It was the creature living in you.

As you thought these things, the voice listened intently.

Soon, you thought, wrapping your arms around your shrinking guts, soon, the voice would stay quiet forever.

I'LL GO WHEN YOU LET ME, YOU FAT BITCH, the voice strained. *I'LL GO WHEN YOU LET ME...*

VIII.

By the fifth day, you went hours-long stretches without the voice and you wondered if it wasn't gone completely. But, whenever you smiled at the thought of freedom, the voice in your guts chuckled.

Your fingers kneaded your belly again and you wondered how much longer you could last. The blizzard slowed and the roads were being cleared. There was food—oh so much food—at your fingertips again. The desire to eat bombarded your brain with sights and smells, tingles of delight electric on your tongue.

The want maddened you so much you sat up in bed. Though you didn't want to after so many days, you took a few steps to your phone but stopped only when you crossed a mirror.

Even with the weight you lost—almost twenty pounds— you were still a big girl. But the sight had you fingering your guts again, hunting, in your madness, the source of the voice as you had done in your dream.

You poked the spot where you remembered the stone-thing had been. It took a few minutes—you began to sink into the certainty that all of it was a product of your collapsing mind—but your fingers felt something a few inches above your bellybutton. It was hard like bone but was, seemingly, connect-ed to nothing.

That it was there filled you with an urgency to be rid of the voice anyway you could. You told yourself to wait a little longer, to starve it out. But, as you thought this, the voice in your guts laughed. The sound was strong, virile, like the never-ending soundtrack to your misery.

On wobbly legs, you went to the kitchen and pulled out a drawer. The utensils clattered on the floor. Hardly looking, you groped until you found the handle of a blunted bread knife. You held it in front of you like a holy relic. Your eyes wavered in and out of focus as you looked over its point and serrated edge.

OH, A BIG BITCH WITH BIG IDEAS, HUH? WHAT ARE YOU GOING TO DO WITH THAT? SLICE OFF A PIECE OF BACON, YOU FUCKING PIG? MAYBE A WHOLE RUMP ROAST.

You gripped the knife tighter. "I'm going to kill you," you whispered, the words dry as parchment.

KILL ME? the voice laughed. *THE GIRL WHO CAN'T TALK TO BOYS? THE ONE WHO LET HER PRETTY COUSIN LOCK HER IN A CLOSET WHILE THAT NEIGHBOR BOY YOU LIKED FINGER-FUCKED HER? THE ONE WHO GETS CALLED PIG-TITS AND CRIES INTO ICE CREAM? YOU DUMB FUCK... GO ON. LET'S SEE IF THERE'S ANY GRIT IN ALL THAT BUTTER.*

Unlike the days, the weeks, or the years before, the voice in your guts made you angry.

With one hand, you gouged your flesh until you found the spot. You pressed the knife point to it and took the handle in both hands and remembered your life with the voice. For an instant, you basked in the flood of cruelty and torment. You hesitated. But, as the knife point eased, the voice laughed at you. Hearing it, you imagined the rest of your life, the decades of enduring this game in your shared body. You imagined your own face and, hanging over it like a translucent mask, was the idol from your dream.

The knife entering you was explosive. Like a shamed samurai, you twisted the blade and yanked it to the side, opening your abdomen wide and spilling blood onto your hands and feet. You let go of the knife and let it ease out of you. The knife fell to the floor and you fell beside it.

The hunger and shock stole your sight, leaving you to dig into the wound blind. Your fingers pushed past the soft warmth of your intestines and searched and searched. You directed your hand to find the source of the voice but all you felt was blood and organs. You went deeper.

There was only pain.

In desperation, you worked your other hand into the wound. More blood and viscera squeezed out from between your arms. Yet, for all your anger and all the laughter in your head, your waning strength was replaced by cold. You wanted to cry but couldn't even do that.

WHAT DID YOU EXPECT, YOU DUMB BITCH? YOU JUST HAD TO LET GO AND YOU WERE TOO STUPID TO LISTEN. EVEN NOW, YOU POOR SAD BITCH, YOU'RE STILL HOLDING ON... THERE'S NOTHING LEFT AND YOU'RE STILL HOLDING ON...

—ETC.—

DEVOTION TO THE DEAD

I.

The birth was a success. The little boy weighed a healthy eight pounds flat and had a tiny crop of black hair. Though the baby came out breached, Dr. Felix was able to save it. He cut the umbilical cord and washed the amniotic fluid off its pink skin. Smiling, the doctor wrapped it in a blanket.

The room was small. Felix had added it to his home after his wife had gotten sick. With his wealth, he'd built her a fully-furnished hospital room with the latest in medical technology. Since her illness, he kept it much the same, though now he'd added a crib that, if needed, doubled as an incubation unit. Felix placed the infant into the crib and was glad he hadn't needed the incubator. This one would be strong enough to survive the trip.

"Can I hold him?" the baby's mother asked from the bed. She looked older than she was. Her features were tired, the weathered skin strained across her face. The plumpness of her cheeks showed she'd once forgone food in exchange for self-abuse. Her thin hair stuck to her forehead like spider webs. In a trembling voice, she told Dr. Felix, "I don't—I just want to hold him a minute."

"That wasn't part of the agreement," he said, his tone even. Dr. Felix looked at her. He was a handsome man in his forties, his frame fitting a paternal archetype, yet there was a razor's edge to his stare. He wasn't annoyed, wasn't angry, but a severity hung about him that even the woman—doped up as she was—couldn't ignore.

"I know, I know," she said, swallowing though her sandy throat made it difficult. "But I just wanted to—"

"Caitlin," he said, adding a tinge of venom to her name. "Need I remind you of our agreement? It had very explicit terms."

"No, I-I don't—I just thought...," she muttered.

Dr. Felix walked over to the side of the bed and the woman shrank a bit. "Your *thoughts* are irrelevant," he explained. "I didn't save your life, nurse you back to health, and spare no expense at either endeavor so you could give me your thoughts. Do you understand? You will be paid, yes? You'll be a very rich woman, right? So—"

"I only wanted to look—"

He smiled down at her. The expression was devoid of warmth. "Why did we make this arrangement, if you cared to look?" he asked. "Why did I find you with a baby in your belly and a needle in your arm, if you cared to look?"

"I was on some heavy stuff—"

"A bargain was made," he said right through her voice. "The terms were set. Abide by them." He stepped away, sighing. She'd come to understand it was an imitation of emotion.

He did them often in their time together. Dr. Felix tried to seem caring, helpful, even understanding. But there was something in his stance, his mannerisms, that made her think it was all mimicry. Like he'd watched people having genuine emotions, studied them, and now pantomimed what he'd seen.

He took a deep breath and exhaled slowly. "I understand this all must seem distasteful," he said, reaching into his pocket. He took out a black case no bigger than a pack of cigarettes. "But think of all you're gaining. You'll never have to work again. Never have to stand on the cold corners hoping the next john won't kill you. And for what? Being treated like a queen for six months. Most people would do much worse for much less, I assure you."

She couldn't look him in the eye. "What are you going to do with him?" she asked.

Placing the case on her lap, he told her, "That is not part of the agreement. Inside you'll find a bank card with a pin number. The money I promised is available. And there's a little something extra. Consider it a parting gift. Don't worry. I can attest to its purity. Use it here if you'd like. You earned it. Now, if you'll excuse me. We must be going." He turned his back to her and went to the infant.

"What do you want him for?" she asked again, looking at the case in her lap.

He scooped the child into his arms. "That was not part of the agreement," he repeated.

II.

Driving through the empty streets, Dr. Felix knew the woman would be dead before he returned. He'd put the purest heroin he could buy in that case and, on the off-chance she could tolerate that large a dose, he cut it with a little bromadiolone.

When he'd found her, she was so strung out, she was hardly a person, barely even an animal. Getting clean, she'd screamed for it, even tried suicide a few times. Once, she died for three minutes before he revived her. But once a month sober, she'd confided in him that it was her fourth try getting clean and that she saw Dr. Felix as a kind of savior.

But he knew he was anything but a benevolent caretaker. All those years ago, he couldn't even save his wife, Ivy.

All his knowledge, all his money, all the priests and holy men and practitioners of the dark arts were impotent in the face of her malady. The medicines made her worse. The surgeries weakened her. And all the prayers and rituals did was transform her into a thing beyond saving. Something hopeless that lived yet had no life, a thing that wore his wife's skin but had none of her soul.

Before long, there had been no place left for her to go. The asylums couldn't save her. Hospitals couldn't understand. Months after she stopped speaking, Dr. Felix decided to place her alongside the other Felixes in the family crypt. The dead judged no one. They wouldn't sneer at what she'd become. They'd see her as lasting proof of her husband's devotion.

Still, he hated thinking of her there because all it did was remind him of how beautiful she'd been before the sickness changed her.

She used to wear the finest clothes, had closets filled from trips to Milan, New York, Harajuku. Now, whenever he brought her a new outfit, he'd see it shredded up in the corner with the other clothes he'd gifted her over the years. Now, all her old skill with the makeup brush couldn't hide the waxen hue of her skin or how far her once vibrant eyes had sunk into her face.

The thought clung to him, as it always did, until he reached the cemetery gates. The groundskeeper had been paid to unlock the gates. He didn't even ask why a wealthy man wanted access to the graveyard every nine months or so.

III.

Dr. Felix parked on one of the paths hidden from the main road and took the baby into his arms. It fussed a little since the sedatives he'd given it were wearing off. The night was cold, so the doctor held the baby to his chest as he stepped onto the hallowed ground, passing tombstones both old and new. He needed no lights. He knew the path by memory.

The family crypt stood over fifteen feet tall with grecian columns serving as the façade around its entirety. The full length of it was big enough for whole families of dead, or, as he often mused, big enough for every Felix who'd ever lived except himself. The steps up to the heavy iron door were overgrown with sprigs of grass, but he'd expressly told the groundskeeper to leave them. Looking neglected, no one would suspect anything was in the crypt other than legacies turned to dust.

Dr. Felix stood in front of the door, adjusting the baby

in his arms. "Sweetheart, I brought you something," he called. Though no sound came from the other side of the door, he knew she was in there, waiting eagerly for his visit.

He took a key from his pocket and unlocked the chains on the door. At the sound of the heavy links, something within the crypt shuffled across the dusty floor. Its husky breath was both fearful and aggressive. Dr. Felix pried open the heavy door and winced at the stench of damp rot that came from the open portal. She'd smelled like perfume once.

When the door was open enough to fit through, Dr. Felix shimmied inside and let his eyes adjust to the dark.

The oppressive smell of the place prodded the baby awake. Its sedated cries were dreamy and weak. Still, they bothered the figure huddled in the corner.

In the dark, it was an emaciated jumble of limbs, filthy nails, and a mess of oily brown hair that encased its head like a primitive diadem. It clawed the air from a corner piled up with ribbons of silk and chiffon.

The baby cried louder.

Dr. Felix cooed at the newborn. "Hush now. Don't be afraid. That's my wife, Ivy. She loves little babies. She wants to play with you. That's all. Isn't that right, love?"

He went down to one knee and laid the infant between them.

Dr. Felix enjoyed none of what came next. The initial sniffing. The infant cries. The feasting. All of it while knowing it was his wife doing it. Sick as she was, those fingers that skewered the infant's new flesh were the same he held when he'd proposed. The lips soon to be covered in gore were the ones he kissed before god and his family on their wedding day. The eyes he used to lose himself in would roll over white and there'd be nothing human about her until the meal was done.

Once it was all finished, her hunger sated, there'd be a brief moment when her eyes showed the same vibrant intelligence that had hypnotized him all those years ago. She'd look at him and her bloody lips would thin into a smile and she'd almost say his name, almost tell him that she loved him before reverting back to that scared thing huddled in the corner.

He'd do anything for those precious seconds, those moments she'd be released from the hells heaped on her. She was his wife after all.

Dr. Felix sat back against the nameplates of his distant ancestors and waited to see the eyes he fell in love with once more as the scared thing in the corner crept closer to examine his gift.

—ETC.—

THE FIRST CUP

There was a deliberate ease to the way Celio's father opened the door. "No rush, but it's time to wake up," Pops said to his lanky fourteen-year-old. Celio hadn't slept at all but laid awake in bed since he got home from school earlier that day.

"OK, I'll get moving," Celio told his father.

Pops nodded and left Celio's door open. His heavy boots clomped off into the kitchen where he opened and closed cabinets and gathered the ingredients for his coffee.

No matter how it was explained to him, Celio always thought it was weird how his father prepared for their hunting trips. Pops treated it like the actual morning, even if it was anything but. His father genuinely slept from afternoon to evening and expected Celio to do the same. Pops ate his breakfast, read his paper, and had his shit like it was any other morning... not the evening.

Though Pops got after Celio for letting his drowsiness show before their hunting trips, Celio never really slept. The monte was full of dangers, his father often said, and sleepy people usually found them all. But knowing what was coming—a fresh kill or his father, agitated, scouring the local papers for a month—Celio could only lie in bed with his eyes closed.

Keeping quiet and playing along was easiest, Celio knew. Once, when he tried to say he didn't like going on their hunting trips, Pops sat him down and gave Celio the "hunter speech" and brought out the scrapbook.

He'd made Celio flip through it. On each page was a photograph of one of their past kills. Looking at them, his father rattled off statistics: dimensions, weights, habitat and territory stats, and, finally, a projection of how much each one ate. "It's about balance," he said, never turning from even the goriest photograph. "They'll doom us all if we don't keep them in check. They never stop eating. Not until we kill them."

Sometimes Celio wondered if his dad didn't just like killing things. Maybe he'd always wanted to kill a man but this was the best alternative.

The smell of coffee brewing got Celio moving and he dressed with a sneer lingering just millimeters beneath the surface of his face because it was a ritual. The coffee was for *after* the hunt.

If they succeeded, Pops would open his heavy-duty thermos and pour each of them a cup of coffee. If they failed, then Pops waited until they got home and poured the coffee down the sink, saying, "We don't deserve it."

Dressing, Celio wished he could drink some of that coffee to perk up but another of Pops's rules was to abstain until afterward. "They can smell the coffee on your breath for a mile," his father always reminded him.

Celio finished and met his father in the garage to load the gear into the camper. In a bid to keep hidden from the neighbors, his father kept the garage door down. He wasn't ashamed, he once explained. Times had changed since Pops was a kid and people were just more sensitive. They'd misunderstand if they saw.

It was a relief when Celio found the bait freezer empty.

"I already got it," his father said from halfway inside the cab.

"You didn't need help?"

"Of course I did, but my baby boy was still dreaming about what's-her-name," his father joked. "I kid, I kid. It wasn't that heavy. You all set?"

Celio shrugged. "I guess."

He wanted to thank Pops for loading the bait but didn't since it might sound like he wasn't fully behind the hunting trips, a family tradition since way back in the frontier days. That wasn't it. Celio just didn't like holding the bait bag—the cold plastic was grotesque to touch and when Celio got hold of the things inside... Celio could gut a deer in less than three minutes but simply holding one end of a bait bag revolted him.

"Already use the can? Might as well stay home if you haven't. If you piss out there, we won't see anything," Pops said.

Celio put on an imp's smile.

His father returned the same expression. "Son, I'll make you sit in your own mess until we come home."

"That means *you'll* smell it too."

Pops imitated Celio's shrug. "I'm an old man. I'm used to weird smells."

###

The ride was quiet. It was partially the errand and partially Celio's age. Celio stared out the window and watched Puentes slip away and meld with the dirt ranchettes dotting the western highway. Farther still, save for the fences and telephone lines, the land seemed untouched. Celio looked at the thick brushland and recalled his father once saying the wilder the land, the better the hunting.

His father drove them to a hunter friend's ranch on the edge of Splitwood just south of Dodd. Celio had been there a few times before. It was good hilly land almost made for their kind of hunt.

When they got there, his father parked next to a little clapboard ranch house with small barred windows. Celio helped his father unload the supplies. From that point on, Celio knew he couldn't avoid handling the bait bag. They had a mile to walk under the full moon rising and there was no way his father could carry the rifles, ammo, the bait bag, *and* that stupid thermos.

Celio got the bottom and his father took the top, which Pops tied with a rope to carry it easier. The way his father tied the bait bag made it look like a corpse—even the bottom of the bag felt like it was a person still cool from the freezer wrapped in thick plastic. Celio had to remind himself it was a trick. His mind was trying to make sense of what it couldn't see.

Together, Celio and Pops found one of the clearings set up for baiting. The trees around it had been trimmed over the years to grow with gaps between them big enough for a skilled hunter to shoot through and small enough that animals felt safe within, unaware of the blind yards away.

Once they dropped the bait bag, Pops told Celio to get a tight hold of the wrapping. His father slit the bag open with his pocket knife. The breeze snuck into the bag, opening the flaps and displaying the contents to the bright moon.

Reminding himself what it was, Celio tried to look away but was instantly transfixed by the bag's contents.

It was beautiful even in death. Its skin was dark despite being days in the freezer. The face was full-lipped, flat-nosed, which matched well with the large, unblinking eyes staring up at the stars. The body, too, was a wonder. Firm breasts, a slim torso, skin smooth except for the blackened bullet holes beneath its ribs. Celio tried to peek between its legs but his father called for his attention.

"I lift, you pull," he whispered, sliding his hands beneath its armpits. On three, Pops lifted and Celio pulled the plastic away, balling it up before giving it to his father. Pops tucked it under his arm.

Pops knelt down and unzipped one of the rifle carriers. He took out Celio's rifle and loaded a cartridge before shoving the empty bait bag into the carrier. He took another handful of cartridges and gave them to Celio. Pops waited for his son to nod he was ready before putting a finger to his lips.

It was time for silence.

His father readied his own rifle, slung it over his shoulder, and put the empty rifle carrier into the other along with the bait bag. Slinging that onto his free shoulder, Pops freed his hands for his rifle. He nodded to Celio and walked to the right.

Celio went left, knowing to go fifty paces before changing his trajectory to the nearby blind built into a thicket of huisaches and retamas. The flowering trees masked their scent. Usually, those walks alone through the dark scared Celio. No matter how many ranches or how many nights, Celio always lost himself in the darkness until the shadows in the trees turned into secret monsters stalking him just beyond sight.

Yet, Celio couldn't stop his mind from drifting back to the bait.

He'd never seen a naked woman outside of magazines swiped from his father. And, he thought, in a way, he still hadn't. Celio felt something stir within but as soon as he did, his father's lessons came rushing in. Even dead, those things were dangerous, their power lingering long after they went cold. Repeating that, Celio tightened his grip on his rifle and marched on.

Celio's father beat him to the blind. It was a plain cinderblock square built with windows on three sides for a good view of the clearing and the surrounding land. For seats, there were two heavy stumps tall enough for a grown man to aim from. They were painful things to sit on for long but chairs made noise and noise was dangerous. The blind's back wall had a thin doorway. The door itself was made of iron bars spread out enough to aim through and not risk a ricochet. In the corner was a rusted metal bar used to further barricade the door if needed. His father called it the "oh-shit-bar" because it was only used when everything went wrong.

They'd never used one, but during the first hunts, his father often told stories of people who had. They hadn't been ready. They hadn't covered their tracks. They hadn't been quiet.

Celio hated the quiet that came next. Hours of dull silence, of the cold and the dark. Sometimes, they'd wait hours orthey'd stay quiet until the next morning with only the vultures sniffing at the bait. Other times, when something did eventually come around, Celio was so loopy with boredom that he'd think it was his imagination.

This time, though, they hardly had to wait for something to walk into the clearing.

No matter how many times Celio saw one, he wasn't sure he'd ever get used to them. The impressive shape bathed in the light of the full moon above.

It took the form of a buck, a big bodied thing with an antler crown and fur that almost glowed with vitality. But, as was the case with them, the mistakes gave them away. Its limbs were too long, the hooves too wide, and the antlers had none of the asymmetry so abundant in nature. Yet, of all the flares of variation, the clearest signs were the eyes. They were like two gold coins set into their faces.

Pops said they knew the differences were obvious, but they didn't care. They thought regular folk were too dumb and too weak to do anything about them. Often, Pops said they'd rule the word if *they* were smarter. "Lucky they're dumb enough to get got by two momos like us, huh?" he'd say.

Through his scope, Celio saw this one was one of the smart ones. It stayed hidden, testing the wind, scanning the clearing, and moving through what it thought were the shadows.

A tap on Celio's arm pulled him away from his scope. Pops pointed to his eyes and nodded—he'd seen it too. From there, Pops pointed at Celio then made a pistol with his fingers and fired. It was Celio's shot. Celio nodded and positioned himself behind his trembling rifle.

His father stuck his hand out for Celio to wait. Pops made a cross with his fingers and then closed a fist—line up the shot and wait for the signal.

Celio understood.

Lining up the shot was the easy part. The buck was so big, Celio had plenty of options. It unknowingly faced the blind and for a second Celio wondered if the golden eyes found him. But the thing moved into the clearing and showed Celio its broadside. He got his crosshairs right behind the buck's shoulder and gave his father a thumbs-up.

Pops placed a hand lightly on Celio's shoulder and raised two fingers—ready!—and let the middle one fall—steady!

Celio's finger hovered over the trigger. His breath slowed. But the signal never came.

His father picked his hand up and steadied his own rifle to better look through its scope.

At first, Celio thought Pops just wanted to study the creature and maybe give advice about where to shoot it. But then he moved his rifle out to the right.

Celio checked his scope. The buck hadn't strayed, though now it was sniffing at the bait, testing its dark hair and nudging it with its foreleg.

Pops took his rifle from the window, placed it on the sill on the blind's right side, and looked through the scope a moment. His father's shoulders shuddered, betraying him.

He gave his son a peace sign—there were two of them—and Celio seized with panic. Just one was capable of chasing them down and killing them if they weren't careful. Two could kill them even if they were.

Grim-faced, Pops put his hand on Celio's shoulder. He held up his finger for Celio to pay attention. He pointed at the clearing. He motioned to himself and then behind him with his thumb. His grip tightened on Celio's shoulder to show the importance of his instructions. He held up his hand, telling Celio to wait, and then pressed two fingers to his own lips. He nodded at Celio and Celio nodded back.

Even if he didn't like it, Celio understood. Once his father gave the signal, Celio was to shoot the buck in the clearing while Pops took out the other. It was a simple plan with plenty of room for error. If Celio missed, they'd scatter, chase the sound, and find them. The same if they were spooked. And even if Celio killed the one in the clearing, the second would be enraged. It would hunt them down until the stars went cold if it got their scent.

Celio got the beast in his sights again and put the crosshairs over its heart. He took long, steadying breaths. Each breath felt like a betrayal because any one of them might send his bullet too high or too low and doom he and his father both.

When Pops tapped Celio's leg, the boy pulled the trigger. The rifle kicked but Celio got it back fast enough to see the buck rear up on its hindlegs and fall over, kicking the dirt. There was a ringing in Celio's ears despite his earmuffs.

On the ground, the buck kicked dumbly as its the limbs changed from those belonging to deer then to wolf then to man until finally settling on some mammalian hybrid. It let out a dying gasp which sounded like a primordial curse.

The space between Celio's shot and his father's seemed nonexistent. But, after taking it, his father was manic and yanked the rifle into the blind. He stripped off his earmuffs.

Celio did the same, asking, "What's wrong?"

"I missed," Pops said, wearing a panicked look.

Celio's eyes widened. Death was coming and it would not be gentle.

They'd run drills for this but now that the time had come, Celio reverted back to being a simple teenager. Vulnerable, unsure, scared.

His father had no time to coach him. Pops thrust his rifle at Celio and attacked the iron door. It was heavy and its hinges were rusted by the elements. Celio hoped the door would shut without protest, but it swung halfway closed before getting stuck. Pops threw his shoulder into the bars twice to finally shut the door.

Celio watched his father barricade the door with the oh-shit-bar. He clutched his rifle and slid against the wall to sit on the ground. Celio couldn't hear his father telling him to be ready. His heart beat so fast it muted everything except for the approach of heavy paws.

As quick as Celio realized what the noise was, the second beast slammed into the hunting blind's face.

With his back to the wall, Celio felt the impact reverberate through him. It felt like the blind would collapse from such a blow. He scrambled. When Celio looked back, a fur-covered arm whipped through one of the windows.

Celio was too low to be caught by it but his father wasn't. The claws snagged his hunting jacket and salted the blind with goose down.

Seeing his father caught like that cleared Celio's thoughts.

He ground his teeth and chambered a cartridge before he threw his back against the door and aimed for the window. Nothing was there to shoot but the dark.

Pops anticipated Celio's confusion and spun him into the corner. Before Pops could say a word of warning, the beast was at the door.

Nothing could prepare Celio for what stood beyond the bars. It had taken on the wolfish shape favored by its kind. Unlike normal wolves, the forelegs were thick like human arms. Its paws were human hands made deadly by three-inch claws. The face had the cheekbones of men but a half-snout and muzzle. As in all its shapes, the eyes were like golden disks shining brilliant in the night. That close, Celio understood the danger wasn't just their speed or strength or ferocity. It was their intelligence.

It pulled its lips back and in a half-bark half-song, it spoke. "Abre la puerta, niño, and I promise it will be quick."

Celio saw pure hatred in its glowing eyes. It wanted to hurt them and worse.

It realized Celio wasn't moving and it clawed at Pops who fell to the floor. He still maintained his grip on the oh-shit-bar despite the thrashing. Getting nothing, the skinwalker grabbed the iron bars and shook them. The hinges squealed and the walls quaked and threatened to bring the blind crashing down.

Through it all, one strange thing kept Celio focused. Pops cursing.

"Shoot the motherfucker!" he yelled. "Shoot it in the fucking face, son!"

Celio lifted his rifle and fired.

The world was a wall of painted spots. The blast took everything from Celio. Sight, sound. He couldn't even hear his own screams. He tried to chamber another cartridge, but something grabbed his rifle and then a hand rested on his chest to calm him.

When the world returned, he saw Pops kneeling over him. His face glistened with sweat and his breaths came in big gulps. The doorway behind him was empty. When Celio's hearing gradually returned, he heard his father repeat, "It's all right. It's all right."

"Are they—" Celio tried to ask but stopped when he saw two motionless feet at the bottom of the doorway.

Nodding, Pops loaded both rifles anyway. He scanned all the windows and, once satisfied there were no more of them, Pops forced the door open. All the shaking loosened the door so much it fell from its hinges as soon as they were out of it.

Right outside the blind was the body though, in death, it had shed its false flesh. It looked like an accountant in his forties with a graying moustache. Celio's father examined it and found where Celio had shot it under the jaw. The bullet had punched through the back of its skull.

Down in the clearing, the one Celio'd shot looked like an older woman, her skin wrinkled though her hair was still dark and thick. He'd gotten her just beneath the armpit and hit her heart. A clean through-and-through.

Celio's father allowed them to put their rifles on safety and sling them over their shoulders once he confirmed the two creatures were dead. The walk back to the blind was quiet and Celio could finally breathe again.

"See, son, that's the risk with that bait," his father explained. "Skinwalkers—"

"Pops, can we just not?"

"Son," he said sternly. "I'm trying to teach you something.

Skinwalkers pick wolfskin because they're a lot alike. Wolves can smell their own pack same as skinwalkers. If you can trap one, you can lure the others. You'll never get the whole group, but still. The only problem is because they've got such strong bonds—"

"Like people?"

His father snorted. "Like a hundred other mammals... People included."

They collected their things. By the time they got back to the truck, it was already daylight and a curious buzzard circled above. They drove to the clearing. His father groaned and said, "They'll help move them at the processing plant, but now we've got to haul three. Oh man, your mother's going to have to walk on my back when we get home."

Pops parked the truck just outside the clearing. He didn't immediately get out. "First thing's first," he said and out came the thermos.

Twisting it open filled the cab with the warm smell of coffee. Pops filled the lid with a still-steaming cupful but didn't drink it. He gave it to Celio instead.

Celio took it. He didn't like the bitter taste but sipped it anyway.

His father smiled. "Enjoy it, son. We've got drills to run when we get home."

Celio almost spat the coffee out.

Imitating his son's surprise, Pops shrugged. "You panicked, so we have to practice. But enjoy the first cup. You earned it."

—ETC.—

GRAND ELECTRIC GESTURES OF LOVE

I.

Verduzco had been in love with Cleo Reilly since he was ten. She came into his elementary school classroom and bewitched him with her blue eyes and red hair. Throughout his school years, he contended with these feelings daily—the town of Four Creeks didn't have more than two thousand people in it—and the constant desire to speak to her, to be near her, made him nervous and shy. Most of Four Creeks took these as signs he was strange.

In high school, he watched her date all the wrong kinds of boys and walk the halls without so much as glancing at him. The town was so small, Verduzco thought, eventually Cleo would have to look at him in a new way. He clung to that hope until Cleo started going out with the Wandmacher kid from San Casimiro, a town fifteen miles down the old highway.

With Ryan Wandmacher in the mix, Verduzco saw his hopes get torn to bits. Cleo and Ryan were in love and it filled Verduzco with despair. He dropped out of school soon after and found a job with Animal Services shoveling roadkill. Sure, he heard the whispers, the rumors. The town thought he was quiet and weird and, most likely, stupid. Not fit to be around decent people. But Verduzco had taken the job to get lost in something that wasn't Cleo Reilly.

He saw her in just about anything. Even picking up half an armadillo—sun baked to the density of a bowling ball—he'd think of Cleo, her blue eyes, her red hair.

It wasn't the ideal life, but Verduzco had money in his pocket and a job to go to every week. The routine, though always a new facet of the grotesque with every outing, helped ease his hopelessness. The department earned his loyalty for that. After some years, things were almost pleasant.

Then, in '50, the men were called to Korea, and Verduzco, along with a few others from Four Creeks, took a bus to Puentes to get a physical and deployment papers.

The bus stopped at neighboring towns like San Casimiro and Gaston. To Verduzco's dismay, Ryan Wandmacher got on his bus and sat in front. Verduzco couldn't help but watch the shape of Wandmacher's head throughout the ride. It made him think of blue-eyed Cleo and her red hair all over that smug head.

At the base in Puentes, Verduzco was turned away. He'd passed the physical and had done all right on the written exam, but the draft officer found Verduzco's smell so repulsive, the officer considered it his duty to declare Verduzco "unable to perform the duties of a member of the United States Army."

Verduzco was quiet on the bus ride back. He was ashamed. He didn't want to go to war with anyone, in truth. He'd never heard much about the Koreans. He was sure they were nice people—except for the ones they were fighting—but he had no desire to see their country or get shot in it. A part of him wanted to be relieved. Another part of him said Ryan Wandmacher had gone to Puentes, had been looked at and examined same as Verduzco. . . except they *wanted* Ryan Wandmacher. They needed brave men. Men like Ryan who could be loved by a woman like Cleo Reilly.

The draft had looked at Verduzco and thought he wasn't fit to serve. Just like Cleo.

II.

By 1952, Verduzco had returned to his routine. The new highway to the Valley had opened and gave him a new stretch of road to clean. The highway brought vitality to the town. New businesses, an extra filling station, and a few more families too. That same year, Verduzco sat in the office across from Chuck Aaron, his boss.

For a while, the only sound in the office was the rustling of newspaper pages as Chuck flipped through the local news. "Well, ain't that a shame," Chuck said. "Local kid, Wandmacher. Apparently, he got killed. On Hill 266. Shit, can you imagine? Dying on something that don't got a name but a number."

"Let me see that," Verduzco said, taking the paper.

Verduzco read the obituary. Wandmacher was to be buried in Arlington National Cemetery alongside other Texans that had "given their lives to help those in a foreign land." Verduzco kept thinking a single notion, one that disgusted and excited him all at once. Cleo was single.

When Cleo and the Wandmachers returned from the Capitol, Verduzco knew his chances were still close to nil. Cleo dressed in black and rarely left the house the hero Wandmacher had built for them. Usually a ray of light in the bleak town, now Cleo dressed for mourning. This went on until the Four Creeks' Winter Festival.

The town hired carnival men and a pit show. They set up a large tent that, for a nickel a person, served as the looking ground of curiosities. Among the strange attractions was a man with teeth filed to points and tattoos from the top of his head down to his feet. Another was an enormous woman with ankles as thick as a light post. Another still was the pinhead who grunted at the crowd and bit the heads off mice from a bucket.

Like most of the county, Verduzco had been there that first night, enjoying a break from monotonous smalltown life. Inside the pit show tent, he spotted Cleo among a group of former classmates.

Two things about her struck Verduzco. The first was that she wore a blue brooch on her black dress. He took it as a sign that the shell of mourning surrounding Cleo was finally deteriorating.

The second—the most profound—was she was laughing.

She hid the laughter behind her gloved hand, but it was genuine.

None of those signs gave Verduzco the courage to even stand beside her at the same display she'd stopped to examine or even exchange the most innocent of pleasantries. She'd smell his intentions, he thought. They'd insult her. Instead, Verduzco waited until she left the display cabinet to see what made her smile.

He was surprised. It was a rack of specimen jars. The formaldehyde almost glowed a greenish amber in the light. A young carnival worker pointed at each jar and told their histories. A two-headed piglet from South Hampton. A set of shrunken heads from Peru. But the one getting the most attention was in a tank that took up a shelf all its own. It was a mermaid.

According to the carnie, it had washed up on the shores of Greece and had been preserved for decades to be shown around the world. Looking close, Verduzco shook his head. It wasn't anything more than a shaved monkey cut in half and stitched to the back end of a catfish. He scoffed, realizing the carnies kept the specimen jars under dim lights so no one could see the stitching, but the people around, though, stood in collective shock. The air around him filled with whispers of astonishment.

Verduzco couldn't believe it. His boss dabbled in taxidermy and rambled about it whenever they scraped an animal that wasn't soup-splattered. Sometimes, Chuck even brought his pieces to work. He liked arranging small animals—racoons, birds, rats, even snakes—in ridiculous poses. Jack rabbits at a dinner table arguing over the bills, a little beer can and tiny pink notices included. Field mice jumping rope with grass snakes. A woodpecker cheating at checkers. He'd even told Verduzco about the ways people used to make two-headed animals and other little cryptids with hardly more than sawdust, thread, and some animal parts.

People paying good money and squawking over something Chuck Aaron could do over a long weekend was ridiculous. But those jars charmed Cleo and that was enough for Verduzco.

III.

The project, next year's deadline, and the thoughts of Cleo's smile at his finished work gave Verduzco an energy he hadn't felt since he first saw Cleo. That morning after the festival, he went to work early. His envisioned project painted every mundane part of his day in new and wondrous ways. He cruised the highways in the county truck looking for roadkill. He wanted the freshest animals because they'd make the best materials, so Chuck once said.

Those next months found Verduzco busy. Mornings and evenings, he scanned the highways, pulling over to examine every dead thing. Sometimes he got lucky like with the horse whose back end had been smashed by a semi. He'd been quick because no one cared about deer or javalinas or ranch dogs, but horses were valuable. Verduzco held its head and felt the bones beneath for any breaks. He massaged the ribs to gauge how far up the fractures went. In the end, the head was salvageable and Verduzco cut it off with a shovel.

The shovel blade was dull and the horse neck thick. He did it fast and messy and, by the end of it, Verduzco was splattered in gore up to his thighs. He placed the head delicately in a bag in the truck bed and drove home. The head went in the ice box with some of his other materials. Verduzco's arms were sore for days after decapitating the horse and he decided he needed better tools if he was going to make a curiosity that could earn Cleo's smile.

From then on, a big knife and machete rode along with him.

The project soon took over his whole work day. When he wasn't out collecting, he was getting an education from Chuck Aaron. Some people would've been suspicious about being quizzed over such a morbid hobby, but Chuck enjoyed the art.

Over coffee and donuts in the morning or tacos in the afternoon, Chuck talked on and on about skin preserving oils, solutions, name brand twine, techniques to slice quickest, and things to avoid. "A rotten liver'll make a bobcat mount stink like a Mississippi whore for a decade," he laughed once.

Verduzco laughed along... and took notes.

He jotted down his notes on the *San Casimiro Sentinel* pages and took the paper home "to finish that crossword puzzle," he'd say. He'd smile when Chuck called him an idiot for spending so long on the same crossword. Verduzco suspected Chuck imagined him staring all night at a stupid puzzle most of the biddies in town finished in an afternoon.

He didn't care, though.

Let Chuck and the rest think he was smelly, weird, and stupid. If they thought those things, they'd continue to leave him with his freezer full of hindlegs and forelegs and torsos and heads. Alone with his tiny house full of bones and twine and sawdust.

IV.

He tried designing his curiosity but found he was even less talented with a sketchpad than with wooing women. At the San Casimiro Library, he picked up art books and drawing books and a few books on native animals of the area. He copied and traced from them until the most beautiful pieces decorated his walls. Verduzco did find their sketched eyes unsettling, though. He felt those penciled eyes judged his work, his dedication. The frustration of being watched bled into his job. The scrapes of the shovel were messier, the smears of guts across the asphalt more plentiful. The hauls to the carcass pit were in silence.

The carcass pit was a hole in the ground on the county line where they threw pieces of animals. It stank of rot and a perpetual cloud of flies and vultures, scared into flight by the truck, hung over it. Chuck leaned against the truck with a beer in hand, talking about taxidermy, oblivious to the pit and all the flies around it.

"—but, as you can imagine, people don't think taxidermy is a noble art," Chuck said. "It used to be the only way to see animals from other places. Stories didn't work. Hell, you go to England—"

"You've never been out of Texas," Verduzco groaned, carrying a pair of dead racoons.

"You don't have to leave Texas to read a book," Chuck countered. "If you were to ever go there, you'll see carvings on the cathedrals. These scaly things with a mane, but the rest looks like a dragon, you know what those are? Huh? Ever heard of such a beast? Well, that's what they thought lions looked like. And why? Because when they were told to carve a lion, they didn't know what the shit one looked like. Taxidermists were goddamn pioneers of information—"

"Then how come people stopped liking it?" Verduzco asked, hoping to shut Chuck up.

"Because some idiots waybackwhen wanted fame so they

made stuff up," he said. "Like that mermaid at the festival. Pur-veyors of knowledge painted as conmen and morbid twits, all because of a few sons of bitches." He drank and thought. "The worst of them was this Italian, Aldani. 1800s, around then. He used to bring the dead back to life. He stuck copper wires up dead animal asses and, like, hanged criminals and jolt them until they danced. He used to tour all over Europe."

"He did what . . .?" Verduzco asked. The thought of elec-tricity gave life to something that floated just out of reach.

Chuck scoffed. "Not only that, they knighted the bastard for it. Can you believe it? Having to call that ghoul 'sir' and bow to him. All for what? Playing dolls with dead stuff."

Verduzco didn't say anything.

"Don't get me wrong, a mount is preservation," Chuck mused. "A snapshot of life. But that shit—it's like going to a five-star steakhouse and playing with your food."

Verduzco nodded but was no longer listening to what Chuck said. A vision was forming, piece by piece, and each one fell into their proper places. All they'd needed was a stage on which to dance.

V.

Verduzco started calling in sick once the weather cooled. Half days. Full days. He went out in the mornings and evenings to scan the roads. But unlike the first months of scouting when Verduzco was just seeing what was available, now he was hunt-ing. A design was in his mind, burning like a vision. All he had to do was find the right pieces.

He had to buy another ice box on credit and ate a strict diet of bologna and canned beans, but all the stomach cramps and stringy shits would be forgotten when Cleo saw his work and smiled.

More luck fell on Verduzco a month before the next Winter Festival. It took the form of a semi plowing into a bunch of runaway cows from the cattle auction at San Casimiro.

When they'd gotten the call, Chuck and Verduzco had expected a mess, but they found a scene like neither had ever seen in their corpse scraping careers. The truck had struck five cows—a pair directly, while only clipping the other three—but the force was enough to pulverize them and scatter meat and limbs all over the highway. A half a torso wedged in the tires. A cow's back end tangled in a barbed wire fence across the road.

Chuck and Verduzco worked all day in sight of drivers and buzzards. Even ripped apart, the pieces were heavy and messy. Dragging the hind legs left a trail of juices and hefting a front quarter had the bones sliding out of the skin like arms from a sleeve. The smell called every fly for a mile and soon they had to tie bandanas over their faces to keep from inhaling the living cloud.

The flies followed them all the way to the carcass pit where they mingled with the others over the bones and rot and the fat blue beetles nibbling the gore. Chuck threw the pieces in a hurry, saying overtime wasn't enough to keep him away from his beer and recliner. Verduzco, too, acted drained, but his selection of the pieces was careful and each time he tossed them, it was near the lip of the carcass pit so he could find them later. Good cowhide and sturdy hooves could serve as a nice base, he thought.

VI.

The air finally turned cold at the close of November. With the festival three weeks away, Verduzco called Chuck and requested more time off. Whatever his vacation days couldn't cover, Verduzco told his boss to dock his sick days too. When Chuck pressed him for a reason, Verduzco said he needed some time to work on things.

"What kind of things?" Chuck asked him.

"Gestures of love," Verduzco said and hung up.

The project was coming together. If it worked, Verduzco thought things might finally change. He felt it was something like destiny.

He'd been born into a little nothing town like Four Creeks so he could meet Cleo Reilly and never have her. Up to that point, he'd thought it was some cosmic joke but realized now it had been for the best. If he'd had her in his youth, he would've been shy and awkward—his pimples or his smell or gangly frame would've made him a passing phase. Even when she went with Wandmacher, Verduzco still wasn't ready, still didn't understand the commitment it would take to get a woman like Cleo.

Then there was the new highway.

There was no randomness to the festival, to the cabinets of curiosities, not even to Ryan Wandmacher's death. Destiny had done it all. It gave him his job with Chuck and had sent those cows running right into that semi. It even made some old European revive corpses a century ago just for him. Destiny made a trillion things happen so he could build his curiosity and show Cleo how much he adored her.

That first morning of his artistic exile, Verduzco turned off the heat and opened all the windows to chill his place to a dry forty degrees. He dressed against the cold with thermals and sweaters and a thick coat and then brought out all the pieces he'd need. He set them–the spools, the thread, the coils of wire, animal parts–anywhere there was space.

In his mind, the pieces arranged themselves before him, the parts rolling across the table and stacking atop one another, the wires snaking into the frozen meat and bones, the needle and thread dancing over the seams like a busy bee. It was there looming in front of him. All he need do was make it.

For all his inspiration, Verduzco found he wasn't very good with the needle and the pieces resisted him. The skins didn't obey the same way they had in the books and manuals. Chuck had described a relatively simple process, but Verduzco struggled until he thought he'd go mad.

He slept only a few hours at a time for nearly a week. He ate to avoid starvation and to keep his hands steady. The only thing to keep him company was the radio and all that did was remind him the Winter Festival was close.

Those were the stories of his days. Toil. Sleep. Toil. All punctuated by radio jingles about the festival.

Three days before, when the trucks rolled in and the tents went up, Verduzco woke out of his trance and was confronted with what had been a vision but was now a reality before him, beautiful and motionless without its electric lifeblood.

He looked upon his creation and wept for it was good.

VII.

The turnout was larger than expected. People from all over the county and as far as Puentes clogged the festival grounds. Verduzco had begged the planning committee to give him a spot inside the pit show. After reminding one member—an old classmate—that he'd never told anyone what he'd seen transpire between his classmate and another altar boy years before, Verduzco secured a spot in the back corner of the pit show.

The morning of the festival, Verduzco went in to set up and to see the competition. The pit show had a bearded woman and two aborigines. They didn't look too awe-inspiring—the bearded woman did laundry while the aborigines read dog-eared paperbacks. The least impressive was the cabinet of curiosities. A two-faced cat. A hand with seven fingers. A frog with snake fangs.

Verduzco smiled. Next to them, his creation would be like the breath of the gods. But to his dismay, once the people arrived, they fawned over the smelly jars and obvious needlework.

He'd built a little stage for his creation so it could be better viewed and to hide the wires that ran up its back like ivies. Behind it, Verduzco set switches and record player. His creation needed music to dance, otherwise it would just be dead animal parts jerking around on a stage. It needed to be beautiful so Cleo could smile those black clothes right into a trashcan.

Verduzco kept the strung-up curtain closed for so long his fingers cramped. For hours, curious children and couples hovered just outside the curtain, pulling at it to peek inside. All they found was Verduzco hissing them away.

Late in the evening, he spotted Cleo in the middle of a gaggle of people. She wore a dark gray dress and coat. As if the gray—so much more inviting than black—weren't enough reason for Verduzco to get excited, she wore a bright red cardinal brooch. Verduzco bit down on his lip at the sight of it. He knew what *that* color meant.

He waited for her to get closer to the curiosities before opening the curtain to reveal his stage. At first, people only saw the general shape of Verduzco's creation. The mystery drew people in, including Cleo and her friends, to see what new attraction the festival offered.

Verduzco turned on his record player and the gentle strum of a guitar overcame the whispers and drunken barks and then Bingo Grosbeak crooned "Baby, I Miss That Smile."

Verduzco hit the lights.

The crowd gasped like Verduzco knew they would. It was the first time, he figured, some of them had ever seen something made with pure love. But they'd only seen the shape, the body.

He connected the cables to a car battery. The stage lights surged, Bingo skipped, and then the creation danced for the crowd, for Cleo.

The base was a set of curtsying cow legs covered in bobcat fur and turkey feathers sewn to a pig's torso. It wore a patchwork vest of skunk and possum pinned shut by bird legs painted the blue of Cleo's eyes. Each arm was a pair of deer legs positioned so that every jolt of electricity brought the hooves together like clapping cymbals. The face was a javelina's stretched over a horse skull. It smiled with a mouth full of flat cow teeth. What spaces the javelina skin couldn't cover, Verduzco filled with jackrabbit ears and vulture feathers. He'd nailed an old stovetop hat on its head. The nails looked like christ's crown on its head but were the only way to keep the hat on when it danced.

Once moving, the creation silenced the crowd. They watched it clap its hooves together with a sort of hypnotic reverence.

Verduzco snuck around the stage to watch the reactions, one especially. The angst and aches drained away once he saw Cleo's face, her eyes wide and beautiful lips opened—just a little—in awe of his grand gesture, but Verduzco couldn't enjoy the moment long.

Bingo's voice slowed to a palsied pace.

Verduzco looked in time to see some of the lights burst in a shower of sparks. One of the legs glowed red before a tongue of flame erupted from its thigh, catching some of the pelt vest on fire too.

Verduzco took the coat off his shoulders and ran to his creation. He swatted the fire until it was only embers, but the acrid smoke scattered most of the crowd. Through it all, the creation danced, grinning and watching with marble eyes. Of those who had seen the curtain open, all but one clutched their noses and backed away from the stage.

Cleo Reilly stared at the dancing creation as if entranced by it.

Verduzco took a step toward her. He imagined all the things he would say, fantasized about how she'd be amazed at his dedication while, at the same time, she'd be embarrassed that he loved her for years yet would be moved by his grand electric gesture of love.

The closer he got, the less he could trace any of the grief he'd seen in her since her widowhood. "It's all for you," he wanted to say, and she would listen. She'd think it was sweet and would fall into his arms in front of the whole county–even in front of the remaining Wandmachers. The people would see he wasn't a nobody. She'd fall into his arms and tell him he was her man.

Verduzco opened his arms to accept her embrace and Cleo Reilly violently vomited onto his boots.

–ETC.–

A WHISTLE IN THE DARK

I.

Something broke in Domingo Halcon the day his son got lost in the monte. There was no great mystery, for himself or the public, who was to blame. The boy, Polo, hadn't wandered off. No one kidnapped him either. The boy had been lost in the monte for six days because Domingo left him there.

All he'd wanted to do was teach Polo a lesson. His son had been a terror for hours, screaming, demanding, and kicking the back of Domingo's seat like the boy was stomping a colony of ants. Polo cried like he was on fire. Domingo had told his son to stop. His wife, Ana Cristina, threatened to spank Polo right on the highway. Still, the boy wailed and fought.

"That's *it*," Domingo had yelled as he pulled the car over. "You're getting the belt, young man." He met eyes with his son through the rearview mirror and the boy looked terrified. Domingo often thought of that look in his boy's eyes and thought of how monstrous he must've looked to his son.

So terrifying was that look, it sent Polo scurrying out of the car. They'd pulled over beside one of the many ranches lining the highway. The boy ran through the tall grass and reached a barbed wire fence. He climbed over it like a monkey and ran to the brushline, stopping just before going headlong into thorny mesquite and nopales.

The day had been so hot, Domingo remembered, and the heat made him angrier. He walked, undid his belt, and whipped the grass. "You get over here this instant," he screamed. He reached the fence of mostly rust and jagged edges and looked into the boy's eyes. "I've had it! You don't respect me! You don't respect your mother! You cry and whine like you're prince of the goddamn world. But I'll show you, believe you me. You come out of there *now*."

Seeing that Domingo didn't want to cross the fence, Polo had simply said, "No."

"Polo, you get off that land now," Domingo seethed. "You are trespassing, young man. Do you know that? In Texas, little boys can be *shot* for trespassing. Now get out of there!"

Polo gave him a smug look that told his father none of his threats meant a thing. There, Domingo was playing the boy's game, a game he'd played for too long. "I won't," Polo said, his squeal defiant.

"Really?" Domingo told him. "Fine. I'll tell you what, little prince, why don't you stay here, then? Huh? You like it so goddamn much, stay," he said, pointing with the belt still clenched in his hand. "If you get tired of it, the house is forty miles that way. See you at supper."

Domingo walked halfway to the car before turning around and, seeing that Polo hadn't moved, waved. "See you, son," he yelled. Once in the car, he told his worried wife that they'd only pretend to leave. It would shock the boy, he told her. The next turnaround, he assured her, was only a mile away.

When Domingo had to talk to the reporters, he asked them how he could've known the turnaround had been closed or that it would take thirty minutes to get back, not the five he'd expected. How could he have known that the boy wouldn't stay still, frozen in fear? He'd looked in the monte for hours, shouting his son's name, assuring him he wasn't mad. He only wanted to know Polo was safe. With no sign of his son, Domingo had been forced to get the nearby town involved, which alerted the media.

He was ashamed under the glare of the camera lights, but he endured it because the more who knew, the more might come and help look for his son. For the days leading up to the boy's rescue, it was an ominous story, people waiting as time went by to hear of a little body being found. So, when the boy was found on the sixth day, the whole world seemed to be watching. And the weight of that attention was on the boy who'd survived, many said, despite his horribly irresponsible parents.

II.

Polo didn't speak at all for three days after being rescued. He was examined by doctors and pathologists and psychiatrists but, surprisingly, nothing was wrong with the boy other than having lost a pound or two. People thought it was a miracle he survived the cold nights and the hot days in such unforgiving terrain. There were snakes and smugglers and wild dogs in the monte, any of which wouldn't've given much thought to hurting a lost boy.

When Polo finally did speak, the whole world seemed to be listening. He said he'd cried and ran into the monte and got lost. He followed a path, thinking it would get him back to the road, but all it did was lead him deeper into the brush. Scared, Polo had wandered until nightfall. He slept under a tree. In the morning, he found a ranch house with the door unlocked. Though there was no food, there was a working faucet to drink from. Polo said he waited there until he heard the search teams combing the land.

The whole world was sympathetic to his horrible adventure and showed it with a shower of toys and clothes and scholarships. They gave these things, thinking those trinkets and checks would somehow compensate the boy for being born to terrible parents. The same went for the reporters who praised Polo's bravery while wordlessly calling Domingo and Ana Cristina monsters.

Domingo said nothing. He understood.

He understood when the talking heads howled with rage that he and his wife weren't charged with any crime. They cried neglect and abuse and some even called it attempted murder. They wanted Polo taken away as if Domingo waited for his son with a bullwhip, ready to beat the boy to death for embarrassing him. For a week, he was the national example of what was wrong with modern parenting and the modern legal system. Petitions were passed around. Features on websites devoted to people like Dolores Guarecuco and The Pig Man.

The world thought Domingo was scum and every time he saw the way Polo acted after his week in the monte alone, he understood why.

Polo wasn't the same hyper child. Before the monte, he was perpetually bored and aggressively sought out solitude. His parents annoyed him and he avoided them at all costs. But, after his return, Polo was never out of their sight. Wherever his mother went, he either positioned himself to be able to see her or outright followed her into rooms. Even when in the bathroom, Domingo and Ana Cristina could see the shadows of Polo's feet under the door. He watched them in silence whereas, only weeks before, any time around his parents was filled with obsessive questions or outright complaints.

For weeks, his father wanted to sit down and talk to him, not to try to justify what he did but just to listen. To try and help Polo understand what happened, what he endured. But as much desire as Domingo had for dialogue, he didn't have the strength to actually approach his son.

The shame of his cowardice mingled with his guilt over leaving the boy and took a toll on Domingo. Soon, as if trying to atone by reliving the boy's suffering, Domingo ate little and hardly slept. He stayed up for hours, the television on though he wasn't watching it until Ana Cristina kicked him out of the bedroom. The tv light gave her strange dreams, she said.

Domingo spent his nights in the living room, eyes open and mind shut inward. On one such night, blindly skimming the channels, Domingo heard a whistling between the ebb and flow of programs. He followed the sound through the darkened house until he reached the source. The whistling came from Polo's room. Domingo stood there a moment. He knew he should investigate but was still too ashamed to brazenly enter the boy's room.

After a moment, he opened the door just enough to look inside. Polo stood at his open window and looked out into the night. He was whistling a familiar tune—the theme song to one of his cartoons. But they weren't the bored notes of a wandering mind. Polo whistled with a deliberateness Domingo was not prepared for at that hour.

Domingo watched his son a minute, the boy whistling half a tune and then waiting before starting again.

"What are you doing, son?" he asked. The suddenness of his voice in the silent house made Domingo wince, thinking he might frighten the boy again, but Polo was slow to react.

"I'm calling the bird lady," Polo said, still looking out the window.

"The bird lady?" Domingo asked from the doorway. "Who's that?"

"She kept me safe in the monte," Polo said, finally turning to his father. "She gave me back to you."

III.

The next morning, while Polo ate cereal and toast and jam, Ana Cristina questioned him about the bird lady. She too felt guilty and tried to broach the subject without accusation. "She sounded... nice," she added nervously. "I'd like to thank her for keeping you safe."

Polo smiled with a mouth full of cereal. "She was real nice," he said. "She let me stay with her until you looked for me."

"Why didn't she try to find us?" Domingo asked, voice soft as velvet. "I'm sure you told her we were worried."

Polo looked at his father with a stare that scrutinized him beyond what a boy of his age was capable of. "But... I didn't know you were worried."

Domingo had to look away and pretend to sip his coffee.

"When she heard all those people going through the monte, she told me to go to them," Polo went on. "I wanted her to come with me, but she said it was real important that no one found her, so she said not to tell anyone about her."

"You should've told us," Domingo snapped. He shrank away and expected Polo to recoil at his tone.

"I know, Dad," Polo said. The mention of Domingo's title worked on the man like pleasant music. "But she made me promise not to tell anyone. Even you."

Ana Cristina looked at Domingo and back to her son. "Why would she do that, honey?"

"She said she doesn't like people," Polo replied. "She likes babies and kids but not people. That's why she only goes out at night, so no one sees her."

"Did... did you find her house?" Ana Cristina asked. "Is that how you met her?"

"She found me," the boy said. "It was dark and I was cold and hungry"—each of Polo's words made his parents feel as though weights were being lowered onto their necks—"and I was crying and it was dark. Dark *dark*. Then... she whistled. She whistled 'Dog Pound Detectives.' I heard it and yelled, but she didn't come. She whistled again so I whistled back. And then she came and got me and took me to her house."

"Did she tell you her name?" Ana Cristina asked. "Mommy and Daddy—"

"She said names are secrets," Polo interjected.

"Well, uh, what'd she look like?" Domingo asked. Inwardly, he berated himself.

Polo stopped to think a moment. "She looked like an old lady with all these strings and necklaces and feathers and they were—wait!" Polo scooted his chair out and hurried to his room. "I drew a picture!"

Ana Cristina and Domingo huddled together and debated whether or not to press Polo further. Whether or not to call the police.

"Here it is. I drew it for when she visits," the boy announced, bringing a colored sheet of computer paper to the table.

"When she visits?" Ana Cristina asked, taking the picture. "When..."

"All I have to do is whistle and she hears me," the boy said, beaming, unaware that his mother's face had drained of color. "I hope she likes it."

Ana Cristina passed the drawing to Domingo and it nearly crushed his soul.

The drawing was childlike. The woman looked like a vagrant in rags. Her stark white hair fell all the way down past her waist and framed an emaciated face comprised of a hawkish nose and jutting cheekbones. Her eyes were too large for her face and Polo had colored them gold. Her rags were a jumble of feathers and filth and strings tied to things so small Domingo couldn't decipher them in his son's drawing. But they hung all over her, from her arms, her neck, from beneath her clothes. Domingo imagined seeing such a person emerge from the monte in the middle of the night. He comforted himself by thinking the ghastly features were because his son lacked artistic talent.

"Do you think she'll like it?" Polo asked.

"She'll love it," Domingo answered, half paying attention. Something of himself was being lost in the crayon-gold eyes.

IV.

Domingo told the police about what his son had said. When they checked on the boy's story, the police said no one lived on the property. It belonged to a development firm that was sitting on the acreage to eventually turn a profit. Any constructions on the land would've been destroyed and anyone living there would've been evicted a decade earlier. At first, the boy's parents weren't sure what to do with that information. But, soon, Domingo thought the story of the bird lady was... natural.

The boy had been alone, lost, surrounded by dirt and thorns. He'd been hungry and cold and delirious with fright. In times like that, Domingo felt he could understand the boy pretending there was some matronly figure there to help him survive. But, with those thoughts, came the visions of his son huddled inches from snakes, without tears left to shed, whistling to himself just to hear anything other than the oppressive silence of the monte.

So, during his sleepless nights, Domingo excused the whistling. Each note, he felt, was like a sort of prayer to whatever powers allowed his son to survive. Some nights, Domingo stood at Polo's door, listening to the half-tunes the boy sent out his window. Domingo listened as though there was something important in those songs, something to be cherished.

One such night, Domingo heard the whistling start up and he crept to the door to listen. The little songs started the same as they always did—a few bars followed by silence. He listened for a few minutes, but, once the boy whistled for the sixth or seventh time, the boy stopped, cheering, "Yay! I knew you'd come. I kept calling just like you said."

The words wounded Domingo. They reminded him the boy's imagination—not his father—had saved his tiny psyche. At that moment, Domingo was filled with such a profound paternal instinct, he lost his fear and hesitation and wanted with his whole being to open the door and embrace his son.

"Pos claro. Siempre te voy a contesta. Somos amigos, no?" a voice said from inside the room.

The air froze in Domingo's lungs. No matter how he altered his voice, Polo couldn't've spoken those words. The speaker sounded like an ancient woman dabbling in a new language. Domingo opened the door and a maddening din of beating wings confronted him, filling the room with a rush of discordant sounds, until he had to cover his ears against it.

He opened his eyes in the silence that followed to see Polo standing at the window. He wore a playful scowl. All around him, dirty feathers drifted to the floor like a light snowfall. *"Dad,"* he complained. "You scared her away."

V.

The Halcon's took their son back to the psychologists to talk about the bird lady. The doctors all said the same thing. She was a manifestation of the boy's imagination, just a coping mechanism born from the trauma of being left alone in the monte. When questioned about the strange voice, one doctor laughed, saying, "Vocal cords are remarkable things. They can imitate all kinds of sounds and children do have a tendency of playing with voices during their cartoon-watching phases."

None of them had answers about the feathers.

Domingo had collected them in a plastic bag and showed them to the doctors, some of whom, in their amateur opinions, didn't think they were the type found in pillows. Most wouldn't even touch them.

Polo maintained his story. The feathers, the voice, they were all from the old woman who'd helped him in the monte. She'd only come to see how he was doing now that Polo was back home. He'd whistled for her and she'd heard him.

"How does she get to the backyard?" Ana Cristina asked. "If she lives near the highway, does she drive?"

Polo laughed at the idea of the old woman driving. "No, Mom, she flies. She's got big wings like a bird and flies to my window."

Ana Cristina smiled at that and told Polo to go and play. She looked at her husband and sighed. "You heard him. Bird ladies flying to his window... It's like the doctors said. It's his imagination."

"Then explain the feathers, Ana."

"He could've picked them up out of the yard," Ana Cristina said. "The neighbor's cat kills pigeons and crows all up and down the street."

Though he didn't believe a word of it, Domingo nodded. Ana Cristina hadn't been in the room. She hadn't heard the booming whoosh of titanic wings. But he could find no explanation that could make sense of what he'd seen. Perhaps all those weeks of stress and sleepless nights confused him. It had been the middle of the night and Domingo hadn't really *seen* anything.

Still, like the guilt of leaving Polo, the thought that his wife and all the doctors were wrong nagged him. Alone at night, the only light coming from the tv, Domingo couldn't convince himself of any of it—he'd been there. But, if it wasn't the boy's brain and a pilfered collection of feathers, if the boy told the truth, then he'd been saved by an old woman that flew like a bird.

Engrossed in this fantastic idea, Domingo heard Polo whistling in his room. Domingo was filled with a mix of dread and exhaustion. He chuckled to himself and rubbed his face. Domingo went up to the boy's door and reminded himself the whistling was how the boy survived. How he dealt with the memories of the monte and memories of a shitty father too impatient to do the right thing.

Domingo opened the door and found Polo at his open window. The boy wasn't surprised that his father was there.

"Hey, son," Domingo said. "You, uh, trying to call your friend again?"

"Uh-huh," Polo said. "You've just got to whistle. It's like a game. First, you whistle. If she whistles back, you answer, and then she'll come."

Domingo smiled to hide the pain. He imagined his son listening to the dark for a savior that would never come. "Can I do it too?" he asked.

"Sure," Polo said, excited. He pulled his father by the arm and set him at the open window which looked out to their backyard with its cinderblock fence and all the undeveloped land behind it hidden in shadow. "Go on, Dad," the boy urged. "Whistle."

Domingo scanned dark for a second before looking at his son again. "What should I whistle?"

"Anything you want," said Polo, beaming.

"All right...," Domingo said, thinking. He whistled the tune of an old radio commercial for a long-closed Chinese buffet. The jingle made him grin. After a moment of silence, Polo told him to do it again. "She never answers the first time," he assured his father.

Domingo whistled again and listened to the night air. But there was nothing. Domingo sighed, relieved, at proof that all this late-night whistling was nothing to worry about. There were stranger ways to cope with a shit family.

Domingo whistled into the dark again and basked in the silence.

Faintly, he heard a bird sing. The tune for a long-closed Chinese buffet. Domingo forgot to breathe. Logic tried to flood his mind, tried to tell him it was nothing, a strange mingling of the boy's playful imaginings and his own newfound relief.

But Polo tugged at his father's arm. "Answer, Dad! You've got to answer," he said.

Domingo hesitated but let out the rest of the tune. The silence that followed had a weight, a presence. It was herald to something, Domingo felt, as he looked over the yard at the dark sky.

Domingo gradually relaxed, thinking, his son's imagination affected his own. He trained his eyes on the dark to prove it to himself again. Domingo looked at his son and tussled the boy's hair.

"There she is," Polo cried.

Domingo looked into the darkness and a scream caught in his throat.

What came out of the shadows wasn't human no matter how hard it tried to imitate one. It had a hunchback of rags and feathers that hid its face in shadow and it lumbered forward as though it shouldered a great weight. Yet, it moved silently, its footfalls unseen beneath its feathered shroud. Within the folds of its garb dangled the outlines of withered things. Furs and leathery scraps and among them fingers and shin bones and jaws with most of their teeth and bones too broken to identify. They clunked gently together as she moved. Between her rags and feathers and fetishes, she wore no clothes to hide her sagging body.

As if sensing Domingo's fright, the burdened creature let glow its golden eyes, huge disks devoid of pupils. Domingo felt the cold figure's attention like a chilling draft. The glow of its eyes lit the deep contours of its face and transformed the wrinkled skin into deep tattoos carved by a careless hand.

Domingo shut the window, got hold of his son, and walked backward slowly. Never had the boy's room—or any room for that matter—felt so vast to him than in his slow escape. Still, Domingo didn't run, didn't shout. Somehow, he thought, doing so would outrage that inhuman figure creeping towards his home.

As Domingo reached the door, the figure appeared at the window. Its bright golden eyes illuminated the figure's face against the glass. It smiled wide to reveal its mouth, tapered and toothless and eerily avian. The figure—its palm and fingers human but the nails were black-tipped talons—tapped on the window and called, "Niño, por favor, abra la ventana."

The boy tried to pull away from his father, but Domingo held him tight. "*Dad*," he whined. "She's my friend. She wants to come inside. Let her in, please—"

"Be quiet and listen," Domingo hissed. "Go to your mother. Tell her to call the police."

"But *Dad*—"

"Don't argue with me!" Domingo barked. "Go! Now!"

The boy's struggles ceased and, deflated, he sighed and went into the hall.

Alone, Domingo stared at the creature's smiling face. Under its gaze, Domingo had to fight to get even the fewest of words out. "L-l-leave," he demanded. "This is *my* house. He's *my* son. Now, leave us alone."

The figure scratched lines in the glass.

"Get away from here," Domingo shouted, the bluster in his voice forced and pathetic. "You're not wanted here. You—"

"Yo vine porque tu a me hablaste," the figure crooned.

"Stay away from us," Domingo wanted to say, but, as the words formed on his tongue, the figure outside Polo's window crashed through the glass and filled the room with beating wings and cackling laughter.

Domingo threw his hands up in a vain attempt to defend himself. The maelstrom of great wings battered his head and body. He punched at random and felt his fists connect against a body of what felt like solid mesquite, but, despite the pain of his fingers and knuckles, Domingo didn't dare relent.

In the confusion, those taloned fingers hooked into Domingo's shoulders, the wounds immediately searing with pain, and his body locked as he screamed. Domingo was pulled off his feet as suddenly as he'd been caught. The force of its lifting him in the air made him think he'd been ripped in half.

Domingo crashed through the room and was flying up into the night sky to the serenade of hacking laughter from his son's savior, a creature that looked like an old woman with the fetid wings of a bird.

VI.

The police searched the neighborhood, but Domingo was gone. Polo's room was a mess of blood and broken furniture. Ground glass covered the floor like ash. Again, Domingo was in the news. Search parties were formed. Posters and flyers printed.

A week later, the county Animal Control office answered a call. Vultures were picking at something large and stinking beside the highway. They found a shattered body, mangled, in a small dirt crater. The coroner examined it—the wedding ring retrieved had Domingo's initials engraved in it—and found the injuries were consistent with a fall from over fifty feet, though there was no structure of that height within miles of Domingo's corpse. An investigation found no planes passed over the area. The coroner did note that the eyes, tongue, and some teeth were missing, but that was written off as the result of birds.

—ETC.—

THE CHICKENS THAT ARE NOT HER CHICKENS

I.

The smell of flowers and their enriched flowerbeds nearly overwhelmed Russ. He covered his face with his hat and started to call for the small shop's owner, hoping to stop her rehearsed greeting, but she was faster.

"Welcome to Mayela's Flowers and Nursery," she said from the back. "We've got—"

"It's Russ Wise, Mrs. Hernandez," he cut in, but he may as well have stayed quiet.

"—everything from azaleas to zinnias and all in between. We got top soil, potting soil, fertilizer—manure and synthetic. There's no better place in Dodd—or the whole state for that matter," Mrs. Hernandez recited. Midway through, she emerged from the backroom with a bundle of long carnations in her arms.

The short, spectacled woman wore iron gray hair down to her hips. "Oh, hey, Russ," she said, placing the flowers onto a plastic sheet spread across the counter. "What can we do you for?"

Russ forced a smile. "Just hoping to get Caro some flowers. Something, you know, cheerful."

Mrs. Hernandez leaned closer and chuckled. "What'd you do?"

Russ shrugged. "You know husbands."

"I sure do," she replied. "That's why I cut my last one loose and replaced him with a newer model."

They settled on a mix of delphiniums, lilies, and roses but, no matter the prodding, Russ wouldn't be upsold a vase. "We've got a real nice one at home so we might as well use it," he told Mrs. Hernandez.

"Bien codo," she accused, knocking on her elbow. "And don't say I didn't try sending you to battle prepared. But don't you worry. Husbands and wives are both idiots when they're fighting. Husbands are idiots for always pissing off their wives and wives are idiots for always forgiving them."

"Let's hope," he replied.

On the ride home, Russ felt guilty about lying to Mrs. Hernandez, but there hadn't been much choice. It was either lie or tell her Caro had gone crazy.

II.

It had been a Saturday weeks ago. Usually, the Texas sun forced itself through the curtains at that hour, but the sky looked like light rain was on the way and the clouds had kept their bedroom dark. The same must've been true for the kids because they hadn't been awake yet. Russ got up to piss and got back in bed to roll around in half-dissolved dreams.

The toilet flush had woken Caro. She got out of bed, used the bathroom, and brushed her teeth. "I'm going to get some eggs for breakfast. I'll wake you when they're ready," she whispered in Russ's ear.

He buried himself further into his pillow. "Thanks, but I'm sure the kids'll beat you to it."

He felt her cool lips on his bare shoulder even after she was gone and then the mattress pulled his thoughts far away. But his dozing didn't last. Frantic hands yanked him back into the waking world.

"W-w-what's wrong?" Russ blurted, eyes squinting to see through the fog of sleep. Once his drowsiness evaporated, Caro's face stared back at him.

They'd known each other since middle school, fell in love on the same summer shift at the Dairy King, and had been married not a month after graduation. They'd had two children and were content to live in their own company on a hundred acres of scrub brush and green stock tanks near the county line. In all that time, Russ had never seen Caro so terrified.

All she got out was, "Something's wrong. Something's wrong." She pulled Russ out of bed and pushed him downstairs until they were on the back porch. Caro kept her robe closed with a shivering hand and Russ yawned in his boots and briefs.

She pointed beyond the porch, but when Russ followed her finger, he still didn't understand.

It was just the chicken coop—an old, converted aluminum tool shed done up with shelves and chutes for collecting eggs—and all around it were the chickens. Hearty hens pecking at the scratch bucket where it lay toppled over.

Russ looked at Caro.

"It's in there," she said, almost whimpering.

Her fearful tone almost had Russ going back inside for his pistol but he figured if Caro survived then he would too. The coop walls had holes bored through them to let in light and air but, to Russ's annoyance, they made examining the inside no easier. When he stepped past the milling chickens, Russ realized this great and terrible thing that spooked his wife was, in fact, so scary that a dozen chickens stood nearby with the same concern they showed the clouds above.

There were no devils or snarling beasts, just a rooster pecked to death. The body was so fresh, ants hadn't gotten to it yet.

Russ laughed at the chickens. "Weren't having old Hank's nonsense, huh? You could've just told him y'all had headaches."

Caro didn't share his laughter. A dead animal was just a reality on the ranch, but when Russ tried to joke it off, Caro shook her head. "Our chickens wouldn't do that to Hank," she vowed. "No, they knew him and they... They... I can't believe you don't *see* it."

Looking at the dead rooster in his hand, Russ asked, "See what?"

Tears rimmed her eyes. "Those aren't our chickens," she hissed.

Later, as a family, they ate breakfasts of cereal and toast with either grape or strawberry jelly. When the kids asked for eggs, Russ was quick to say, "Sorry, kiddos, none today. The ladies just weren't in the mood."

III.

Russ had grown up with more experience with livestock than people. His emotional range was either silent satisfaction at a good day's work or stoic annoyance from a hard one. Never did he see a man deal with someone who not only harbored a crazy thought but was consumed by it. Caro's ludicrous thought that *maybe* someone switched the chickens had Russ running around the property like a tracker from the movies. But there was nothing to find.

On the drive back with the flowers, he decided to treat Caro like an animal, a horse specifically. They were smart and read their rider's emotions in all kinds of ways. A jerky pull, a nervous shift in the saddle, that kind of stuff made horses jumpy. Their brains thought their riders were reacting to a danger they couldn't see. The rancheros always said pretend, pretend so hard the horse believed it too.

So, Russ rehearsed the whole way home. To the neighbors he passed on the streets, strange indeed was it to see him mimicking reactions in his pickup. A pull-away for feigned shock or a dance of the eyebrows for playful interest. Russ even went over a few innocuous lines, changing the emphases and stresses each time he said them.

He felt like a lunatic as he parked his truck with a forced smile that remained for the entire walk to the front door. It felt foolish when he got inside and Caro was nowhere to be found. The house was quiet but Russ expected that—ever since she got rid of the chickens, Caro was stricter with the kids.

Thinking to surprise his wife, Russ figured he'd put the

flowers in water. He got the empty vase from the cupboard, rinsed it out, filled it with water, and mixed in the flora-food powder. He arranged the flowers the best he could.

Placing the vase on the table, Russ thought he heard something outside. The dining room looked out onto the back porch and the ranch beyond—but nothing was there except the chicken coop and, Russ noticed, a stubborn anthill. He'd sprayed out there, but they must've smelled the blood and chicken scraps left over from Caro's episode days ago.

IV.

It was a relief the kids were at their grandmother's place. They were still so young that they didn't even sense Russ wasn't himself or that it was unusual to visit Mima on a weekday. His mother hadn't minded—she'd turn away the pope for those kids—nor did she ask any questions other than if Russ was hungry.

"You've lost weight," she'd told him.

Russ grinned and patted his stomach. "Doctor's orders," he lied because no one tells their mother their wife has gone insane. Folks down in Puentes talked about their personal business out in public. In Dodd, though, marriages were private affairs.

He'd tried to convince himself that *he* was the crazy one, overreacting to what might be harmless imagination. But it was that she had *still* thought about the chickens enough to make the list that made Russ whisk the kids away.

It had been a page from the magnetic notepad on the fridge. Its borders were strawberry vines and the heading GRO-

THE CHICKENS THAT ARE NOT HER CHICKENS

CERIES was on every page. Caro had meant to throw the page away but missed the bin. On it was a list of every chicken by name—she'd been delighted when she got to think them up— and all the names had heavy X's next to them.

There was no way to know if the note was from when Hank died days ago or the night before and Russ intended to find out.

He'd entered the house that day like there was a panther somewhere inside, and even though he'd asked her to stick around to talk, Caro wasn't there.

Going to the kitchen, he'd seen her standing out back near the chicken coop. He'd been somewhat relieved to see her there, standing so boldly, hands on her hips as she looked out at the land.

Smiling and ready to forget her silly hysteria, Russ walked onto the back porch.

He'd had the list in his hand to confront her but it fell and rolled away with the breeze.

Caro turned to greet him. Her red-speckled face beamed a victorious serenity. Piled about her feet was a bucketful of scratch—at that moment, a bloody machete was driven into it like an excalibur. Feathers clung to the leaves of distant trees and decorated the nopales. Around her, chickens lay in pieces, halved and quartered with mindless savagery.

"Hey, baby. Don't worry," she told him. "I got them all. I had to be sure, so I got them all."

V.

No one was upstairs, but judging from the clothes thrown across his daughter's bed, Caro probably took the kids fishing. The property had tanks full of catfish and sickly bass—nothing worth cooking, but it was fun for the kids. Seeing his tacklebox missing from the hall closet confirmed it.

This time, the love-whispers of relief, of normalcy, felt like a siren song. Every particle of him wanted to believe it was over, that the cloud above his family had drifted on. But again, he couldn't shake the unease dancing up and down his spine.

The dread finally relented when Russ found a note on the fridge. It was on the same GROCERIES paper and Caro had written RUSS in big, loopy letters across the top.

> Russ,
>
> I don't deserve such a good man. After my "moods," it's a wonder you didn't throw me in with the looneys at Almeida. I'm better now. I fixed up the coop. Go see.
>
> Love,
> Caro
> P.S. Took the kids.

Russ whistled a long *whew* and grabbed a beer from the fridge. He opened it, drank, and went outside to see what Caro had done to the coop.

VI.

Russ's mind registered what it saw in the coop and didn't try to hide the image as if Russ was a child. It allowed him to see, sparing no detail, but it did feed Russ a thought, simple and strong as the sun.

It's not real.

The grotesque reds of meat, the stark whites of bone, none of them were there. Not the soft smell of death and decay baked to insufferable fumes by the heat. None of it.

As in a dream, he recognized the jumbled pile of limbs as his children. Fishing wire bound their dead wrists so tightly they remained purpled and swollen even in death. His daughter's face was hidden under her brother's body—he lay like the christ off his cross, head upside down facing the coop door. The boy's face was a death mask of dried and darkened blood. The whack that did it was not enough to cleave the boy's skull completely. It split the skin so the wound divided the boy's face in half. Eyes rolled into his small skull, mouth silently screaming, and lips pulled back to show his broken teeth.

Seeing his son's teeth brought a stray thought that next week the boy had an appointment with the orthodontist in Puentes. That simple thought pierced the dreamy veil.

Russ wailed like an animal, full of pain and devoid of understanding, and crawled to his children. He scooped them into his arms and embraced their cold bodies and screamed until his throat felt like it was tearing from agony.

So deep and profound was his suffering, the first machete chops barely registered. They were like the lashes of a switch against a thick shirt, hardly worth his attention, but one swing caught Russ between his shoulder blade and neck. His left arm went limp and he spilled his children to the ground. He turned, unsure, and the next strike on his shoulder left no doubt he was being chopped up like wood.

He managed a tearful look at his wife before the machete caught him on the forehead and he went down. The coop was cramped, its roof low. Caro hacked at Russ nearly a dozen times before he finally stopped moving.

VII.

It took Caro a while to catch her breath. Those kids—whoever they were—had struggled the whole way. And why wouldn't they? She'd found them out, seen them for the imposters they were. The girl had been the easier one. She was so small. And, sure, the boy ran and hid, but his crying made him easy to find. The man took a long time to die but, in death, she couldn't've been more certain it wasn't Russ.

She'd suspected it and, now, she was sure.

Caro filled the coop with hay they kept around for the horses. When there was an even pile covering the bodies, Caro got a lighter from her pocket along with a folded paper. She straightened out the page—a list of her chickens with all their names crossed out. Below the chickens were three other names: fake boy, fake girl, fake husband.

Grinning, she lit the edge of the paper and tossed it into the coop. Fire filled the space fast and the heat made her step back a few yards. After a while, the coop walls glowed, warping, and before long, Caro had to retreat even further.

As she watched, a pinprick on her ankle made her kick her foot. She'd knocked over an anthill, just a circle of dust with a hole no bigger than a sunflower seed. She brushed off her foot and went inside for the bug spray.

—ETC.—

LEONARD AND THE CAROUSEL

I.

The company assigned Tomas to the Riverside Mall and, at first, the idea excited him. He hadn't been to that mall since he was a kid. The storefronts, bright and filled with clothes and toys and gadgets, lit up his memories. The mall's layout nearly unfolded itself in his mind from the Silver Coin Arcade and Sal's Pizza to Canales's department store that hid behind the two-story carousel and its obnoxiously cheery music. Tomas could still hum the tune with ease.

Once, he and his grandmother tried to catch the last feature of some cartoon at the movie theater, but they never made it. Instead, they walked the entire length of the mall in defeat, his grandmother breaking the silence with apologies. Tomas hadn't said anything because he needed no apology. The empty mall was better than any movie.

The main corridor with its high ceilings and avant-garde sculptures of doves floating among tin spheres was for them alone. The storefronts were dark, obscured by their gates, and hid their inventories in shadow. Even the carousel was off. The horses with their white teeth and tails touch-dulled were life-less without the multi-colored lights and happy song. Tomas had imagined breaking away from his grandmother and running through the empty place.

He enjoyed those memories as he exited the highway to downtown Puentes.

What greeted him was not the same joyous building of his memories. Riverside Mall now looked like a blockish beast drudged out of the lazy river behind it. The sign was rusted, some of the bulbs blackened by neglect. The parking lot was more pothole than asphalt and within the ruts were nests of cigarette butts and the occasional syringe. The service entrance Tomas was to use was beside the main doors. Its glass was marred by gang signs and crude declarations of love.

Tomas found the door locked and rang the bell next to it. The dayman, Ruben, took a minute before he inched his way to the door and looked out its steel-mesh window. He recognized Tomas by a photocopy of Tomas's ID and unlocked the door.

The service corridor they walked was drab and smelled of cardboard and cheap disinfectant. The narrow hall was dotted by steel doors for shop deliveries. The security room was tucked away in the hall's center.

Even before entering the little monitor-lined room, Tomas was uneasy. The isolation and decay, he thought, in the right context, were frightening and strange. The dark had that power, he knew. So did the lonely hours he'd work. Yet, what tied all the strangeness together was the old woman waiting for him and Ruben.

Mrs. Maria V. Crawford owned the mall. She was a plump

woman, short in stature, but gave off no air of frailty. Her black eyes were deep, their stare weighty. When she spoke, her voice was surprisingly buoyant and youthful.

"You were informed of the standard duties, yes?" she asked.

"Not really," Tomas said.

"The agency told you nothing?"

"No," he told her. "They just gave me the address and told me to show up."

"That is... unfortunate," she said. "Have you done this work long, Mr. Playas?"

"It'll be one night when I clock out tomorrow," Tomas joked.

"So, Mr. Playas, what exactly is your experience?"

"Truth be told, this is my first week out of training," Tomas admitted. "I had some... career changes."

This too seemed to vex Mrs. Crawford. She lifted her hand to silence him. "No matter," she said finally. "This job does not require much skill. For an hour, you will sit in this room and watch these monitors. If anything odd occurs, call the authorities. If nothing, once that hour is up, you will walk the building. If, again, you see nothing, return and repeat the process."

"Have you had a lot of break-ins?"

"No," she answered, offering no more explanation than that. "As you no doubt noticed, this place is past its prime. More than likely, any thief would target the pawnshop down the road. No, I'm more interested in not incurring additional costs, other than your employment, of course."

"Yeah, with this economy—" Tomas started to say.

"The economy has little to do with it," Crawford corrected. "Simply put, the city has grown outward and the area is no longer fashionable. Now, even the lowliest of anchor stores wants nothing to do with a mall that's 'on the outs' to borrow a creditor's phrase. One day, I suppose, if I were so inclined, I could sell the land and get a hefty profit. But... that brings me to the most important part of our meeting. My son, Leonard," Mrs. Crawford said. The way she spoke his name seemed to drive the air from the room.

"Does he work here too?" Tomas asked.

The silent Ruben fidgeted.

Mrs. Crawford glared at him. "My son is... unable to work. So much of what was canon in my youth is now barbarity. There were complications with Leonard. A prenatal supplement—metathormiacin, it was called—that's what made him the way he is. You see, my son is... unique. Shy. He was born healthy, strong, but his mind never truly developed."

Tomas smoothed his hair. "I'm sorry to hear that."

Ruben groaned.

"Apologies are for tragedies, Mr. Playas," she shot back. "My son is a miracle, a misunderstood miracle. Children with his condition usually die in the womb. But not my Leonard. Not my sweet, curious boy. It was people—with their ignorance and mockery—that drove him into this state and forced my hand. Leonard tried the world and was left wanting. So, I opted for this new arrangement instead. He always loved this place, so I let him wander around at night when no one is here. He likes to look into the shops, play in the arcade, and even ride the carousel. The boy can work it all by himself."

"OK, I'll introduce myself and—"

"You most certainly will not meet my son," Mrs. Crawford said. "People looking at him trigger the old feelings. People made him uncomfortable and still do. I've informed him that you will be here during his playtime and to ignore you. So, if you hear the carousel or see the arcade gate open, it is Leonard and thus no cause for alarm. But I cannot stress it enough: don't *speak* to him, don't *gesture* to him, and, above all, do not *look* at him."

"Did the last guy do that?"

"My lawyers have informed me to say nothing of Mr. Arredondo's *accident*," Crawford said, struggling to rise. Ruben moved to help her, but one stare sent him back to the wall. Standing, finally, Mrs. Crawford told Tomas, "In spite of all I've told you, this should prove to be a very mundane occupation. One hour here. One hour of rounds. Repeat until Ruben opens in the morning."

"Yes, ma'am."

"Good," she said, waddling to the door. "If there is an incident with a thief, you can explain it to a police officer," she said. "Leonard, on the other hand, if he were to catch someone... The bathroom is next to the food court and all the vending machines work."

"I didn't bring any change," Tomas said, patting his clothes.

"That's a pity," Mrs. Crawford said and left.

Ruben opened the door for her and hurried down the corridor to open the rest.

Tomas stood in the guard station and tried to adjust to the vast and empty solitude. The walls of monitors served as a reminder that Riverside Mall was once the third longest in Texas. One screen showed the carousel at an odd angle and Tomas remembered that he wasn't alone.

In that giant building, it was just him... and Leonard.

II.

Tomas was anxious that first night. The thought of making the rounds in the dark with a socially inept recluse made his shoulders tense. The monitors didn't help. Their lack of color and sound mixed with the shadows of the storefronts and kiosks made everything look sinister. All of their angles were off-center. Tomas thought it was a way of letting Leonard move around without being seen. That realization made his anticipation worse.

At the top of the hour, Tomas took a series of deep breaths and walked into the main corridor of Riverside Mall. What was left were the scraps of commerce. The benches were square slabs of reclaimed planks painted a sticky blue and the rectangular pots for mid-mall plants were filled with cancerous fiddleleaves and cigarette butts mixed with stale dirt. Some of the gated storefronts, Tomas realized, had been closed long before he ever got there, their innards vacant except for the shells of countertops and the bones of display racks. Empty places with signs from a dying era, copies of a copy of a copy, until there was nothing left but their distorted remains.

One such place was J & B Toys. Its sign was a smiling train and from its smokestack puffed the store's name in a font popular twenty years ago. From what he saw, the toys—teddy bears left to die in piles and a wall of discolored heroes with misspelled names—were either entirely generic or plain knockoffs. Tomas used his flashlight to see a stack of off-putting baby dolls in back of the store. Even from that distance, Tomas felt the itch of their cheap fabric.

Another place, which replaced a long-gone Zoinks!, was a sporting goods store where, for all the time Tomas stared into it, he couldn't find a brand name on any of the equipment.

It depressed him to see Riverside in such a state. His boots crunched on broken tiles and he dodged more than one "construction" area—open holes in the floor taped off with plastic ribbons anchored by trashcans. But, as he neared the eastern wing, a faded sign brought a smile to his face.

The Silver Coin Arcade.

All the old memories of pumping quarters into the *Koth-Dar the Barbarian* cabinet or firing off round after round in *Classroom of the Dead* made him nearly run to it. Though Tomas knew what kind of place the Riverside Mall was now, he hoped somehow, by some miracle, the arcade had been spared by time. The smell of its carpets and walls dashed his hopes away. A stale stink of mold and cigarette smoke left to moisten in the humid air wafted through the lowered cage door.

Some of the games were still inside, the few remaining game cabinets discolored and chipped, but they'd been replaced mostly with slot machines and video poker. Tomas lingered, hoping to glimpse any game of his youth but was disappointed again. He turned away and, knowing no one would care, lit a cigarette. The smoke couldn't make Riverside Mall any worse with its coin-operated rocket ships half destroyed and its lone surviving restaurant—Pizza & Beer—stinking of congealed grease and farts.

He didn't see or hear Leonard that first night. Riverside, seemingly, only showed the vague shadows as though wanting Tomas to mourn what had once been. Still, he kept his mind sharp, ready to stop at any strange echo or whispered word.

III.

It wasn't until the fourth night that Tomas had any evidence of Leonard.

On the sixth hour of his shift, Tomas stood at the front window of Babette's which, from the merchandise, catered to the slutty but economical grandmothers of the area. After lighting a cigarette, he noticed one of the potted plants had been dug up. The soil and cigarette butts were scattered on the floor and they'd been arranged in an almost childlike way. Simple shapes. The sun and moon.

Further down the main corridor, dirty handprints smeared the walls and smudged the display window of a jewelry store. Their cubic zirconia and glass pieces glistened like distant stars. Further still, one of the store's gates had been lifted enough for someone to squeeze through.

In the heavy silence, hangers clacked on their racks and heavy feet slapped on the tile in the dark. Something in there laughed, throaty and buffoonish.

Tomas froze.

It wasn't the jubilant laughter of a thief collecting loot but of a child overjoyed to have found some shiny bauble that might entertain them. Yet, there was a raw power to the sound, a strength in its childish unpredictability.

Careful not to make noise himself, Tomas backed away slow. As Mrs. Crawford had told him, all he had to do was make the rounds and leave Leonard alone. If it was a thief, he'd find out about it on the next pass. If Crawford got mad, he'd say all he did was follow her instructions.

Tomas watched the monitors diligently back in the surveillance room. Even the hint of movement sent him face-to-face with the greasy screens. But the angles were frugal with their secrets. He didn't see or hear Leonard again that night, though now his rounds were exercises in dread, each step a false herald to Leonard's idiotic and powerful laugh.

IV.

Two nights later, Leonard followed him. Tomas had patrolled from the center of the mall to the carousel which was painted to resemble a circus tent. It was as savaged as the rest of the mall. The horses were tattooed, the brass torn off their saddles and hooves, their noses rubbed free of paint. The old scenes painted on the inner walls were hidden in tagger-scrawl.

Tomas thought he'd heard something, a scrape against the metal of the two-story carousel, but paid it no attention. The carousel was old and abused, decaying a little each day until all that would be left were wooden carcasses flecked with paint.

Tomas had made a ritual of his patrols. Since no one had said anything about his smoking, Tomas lit a cigarette at either end of the mall and enjoyed it on the way back to the surveillance room. That night, Tomas stopped in sight of one of the entrances, the light pollution seeping into the hall like a limp tongue. Outside, his car sat alone in the parking lot and the river flowed on.

He smoked his cigarette slowly, watching the glow of the moon surf on the river. The cherry singed the filter and Tomas stubbed the cigarette out on his heel. As he did, a shape receded behind one of the rectangular pots in the main corridor. Tomas saw little of the shape, but it had the dimensions of a person. Tomas knew it was Leonard and didn't look back. Any junkie thief would've clubbed him to sleep already. Tomas continued his rounds and kept his strides even, calm.

But if Leonard saw Tomas's face, he'd know, even in his condition, that Tomas was terrified. Now, all Tomas heard between his steps were the soft pads of bare feet hurrying from shadow to shadow. He thought of what it must be like to be as isolated as Leonard. In rehab, Tomas learned that sometimes solitude helped ease a troubled mind. Yet, in others, it further degraded them.

Tomas tried to put a positive light on Leonard's curiosity. He thought, perhaps, Leonard was like a puppy sniffing behind a new visitor. The thought made breathing easier until Tomas remembered that even if Leonard followed him out of curiosity, Leonard was still very much human and, as such, had a natural proclivity toward the deviant like himself.

Maybe, Tomas thought, Leonard followed to see if he touched a favored plaything or otherwise disobeyed some unspoken rule of the house. Or, Tomas panicked, Leonard's state of mind might be toward the violent, toward ideas that would have Tomas pinned face-first on the floor with an idiot's fists breaking his bones and all the screaming would make Leonard pound harder and harder until Tomas needed to be airlifted to

San Antonio or Houston to be put back together.

His imagination threatened to drown him. It made Tomas's entire being endure the primal struggle between survival and reason. Every cell wanted to run at the grunts formed out of Leonard's mouth, wanted to jump at every treble-filled breath, yet Tomas told himself to walk slowly. Calmly. Leonard, by all accounts, was like a pet tiger. Like all captive animals grown accustomed to people, Leonard was calm but unpredictable and dangerous.

Tomas reacted to the service hall door the same as seeing salvation. Still, even when the door was closed behind him, Tomas didn't sprint for the surveillance room. If Leonard was a wild beast-man, even the sound of retreat might start a rampage. So, Tomas made his way to the room slow and opened the door as if he were bored.

He kept his ear trained for it, but the service door never opened.

Tomas locked the door and didn't leave until Ruben relieved him the next day.

V.

Leonard was bolder the next few nights. He never stood in plain sight but was louder and sloppier in his trailing. The full weight and strength of his limbs were present in the sounds of his observations. Throughout, Tomas kept his pace and his hand on the company nightstick though he knew it would do him little good. Every scenario of Leonard's attacks ended with Tomas's death. Usually a horrible one.

During one night, lighting a cigarette, Tomas caught a glimpse of Leonard in the reflection of a mirrored column. For the nights afterward, Tomas held his nightstick so tight he had to ice his hand at home. It wasn't his own morbid imagination now. He knew Leonard's dimensions.

Mrs. Crawford said he was special, shy. Tomas had thought it was due to a stunted mental age. But the deformities hadn't stopped with Leonard's mind. They seeped into his limbs. After seeing him, Tomas understood why the cameras were at such odd angles.

The bulbous skull and crooked maw. One small arm pressed to his chest as if injured and the other was twisted but strong. All of his visible skin was patchy and gray and Leonard moved like an ape, the large arm leading and the deformed legs slipping behind.

But, as crippled as Leonard seemed, Tomas knew the truth. Leonard was a threat. The man—isolated from society and its concepts of boundaries save the most primal—could do all types of things to Tomas against his will.

Through it all, Leonard never ventured close enough to touch or be seen. Yet, he was always there.

At the end of one shift, Tomas asked Ruben about Leonard.

"Just don't look at him," Ruben said, shrugging. "He won't do anything—"

"And he's running around all night, following me," Tomas went on. "He's followed me—"

"I used to have your job," Ruben said. "Leonard is ugly but harmless. Just leave him alone. If he follows you, it's because he's curious."

"About what?"

"He's like a dog," Ruben answered. "He just wants to know who you are. In time, he'll get bored and leave you alone."

Tomas nodded and went home to soak his cramped hand in ice-water.

VI.

Ruben had been right. After a week, Leonard didn't hound Tomas on his bi-hourly patrol. It seemed Leonard found him as boring as all the other security guards and went back to terrorizing the mall in his own harmless way.

Leonard squirmed his way into the toy store one night and overturned the bin of teddy bears. Tomas heard his brutish laugh throughout his entire patrol. On another, Leonard managed to turn on one of the games in the arcade. Tomas patrolled to the brief tunes of 32-bit glory cut short by sounds of loss and Leonard's frustration. But, most nights, Leonard just played on the carousel.

Tomas never saw the carousel in the surveillance room since the cameras only caught the edge of its canopy. But Tomas heard it. The cheap circus music scratching through worn-out speakers, the squeak of gears, and Leonard's laughter. Full of sound and fury as Leonard's joy was, Tomas couldn't help but hear a twinge of innocence in it. Perhaps it was Leonard's glee that Tomas felt somehow matched his own when he'd ridden that carousel as a boy. Or, maybe, it was how Ruben had explained it.

Leonard was basically a puppy, not inherently good nor evil, just a creature of reactions. Prone to fits of overpowering emotion, there was a bestial quality to Leonard's intelligence but no malice in it.

More and more, Tomas pitied Leonard Crawford, the harmless but forever shunned. Ugly but kind, drawn to the meeting places of the public but only when they were gone, leaving nothing but the ghosts of their scents. Tomas thought the world was particularly cruel then. Leonard was a perfectly fine creature confined to the decaying Riverside Mall for nothing more than the comfort of the masses.

If only they heard him laugh, Tomas thought. At first, as it was with him, the sound would be frightening. The sheer palpability of it was seldom heard in daylight. But if they could only listen—really listen—Tomas knew they'd feel its warmth and innocent joy.

It was infectious. Not that he ever dared join in—in fact, Leonard hid whenever Tomas got within fifty yards of him—but Tomas listened and grew to admire the laughter. Soon his admiration turned to envy.

Tomas used to laugh like that. Used to look at the world like it was built on magic. Life stole that from him, though Tomas couldn't remember exactly how. Ex-girlfriends took some of it with them, a few by force. School took another along with a sizeable chunk of his wages still. Work stole the rest, grinding away the days, gnawing until weeks slid by with nothing to show for it but more bills and neck pain from a shitty mattress Tomas couldn't afford to replace. Tomas had tried to find that magic again with booze and smoke, but they'd only left him twice as empty and twice as broke. But not Leonard.

Leonard had learned enough of the world to hide from

it, memories of scorn still fresh in his simple mind. Leonard's life was frolicking through the garbage of visitors like they were relics of his home world. Still, Leonard laughed with his entire being. All over a carousel he'd ridden for years.

In the surveillance room and on the way home, Tomas tried to recall a time he was ever happy enough to laugh like that. The fact that he couldn't stung him for days.

VII.

Tomas got it into his head that seeing Leonard play on the carousel would somehow transfer some of that childish joy into him. Enamored with the idea as Tomas was, he still knew Leonard was dangerous. But all he needed was a quick look at Leonard's happiness. To do so, though, Tomas knew he'd have to be quiet.

It took days of deliberation to convince himself to do it. A part of him said the laughter was Leonard's private matter, but the thought was demolished by Tomas's selfishness. He—the world!—needed the unbridled positivity hidden away at Riverside Mall. All Tomas had to do was witness it and accept it like a virus. The world would be a better place if he had a look at Leonard in his moments of pure joy.

For a week, Tomas only left the surveillance room when the circus music came on, though he only walked close enough to see the lights play across the storefronts. Yet, one night, Tomas couldn't resist the music's call.

Tomas removed his boots, felt the grit through his socks, and stepped a few times to test the silence. Next, he lit a cigarette and puffed at it until the cherry was bright and strong. Tomas left it burning in one of the potted plants. He thought if Leonard was like an animal, the smoke's smell might deceive him long enough for Tomas to get close.

In the distance, the carousel echoed with Leonard's laugh and it's off-beat percussion.

As Tomas got closer, the carousel revealed itself by centimeters, mere glimpses of the colored canopy at first, then the poles and the faces of horses. Defiled as they were, they kept a steady pace, the gears all greased and in working order. It took Tomas a moment to spot Leonard. Tomas thought he'd find him at the bottom, his disfigurement not allowing any seats beyond those.

But Leonard was resourceful and Tomas saw him on the second story in a two-seater shaped like a carriage pulled by a thick-necked Clydesdale. Leonard raised his misshapen arm as though holding a set of invisible reins, snapping the imaginary leather to urge his steed through some childish adventure playing in his head. All this brought forth the laugh Tomas wanted.

Tomas stepped closer and stared at Leonard's face, eyes semi-closed and mouth gaped open like a wound. His joy revealed yellow, twisted teeth. Yet, Tomas saw through the asymmetry of Leonard's features. He saw no skin color splashed over Leonard's cheeks. Paid no mind to the disproportioned skull. All he saw was joy, pure as the universe. It was a thing no amount of money or drugs could replicate.

The carousel's revolution hid Leonard from sight and Tomas was filled with what he was convinced was the grace of charity. In flashes, he imagined the next few months with

Leonard. The gaining of trust and the start of their friendship, all because Leonard saw that Tomas wouldn't look away, wouldn't treat him cruelly. Tomas could teach Leonard to speak and Tomas would, after many discussions, reveal to Leonard that it was the simple joy he displayed on the carousel that inspired Tomas to be a better person.

These imaginings filled Tomas with a sleepy warmth. A sense he'd found a path to be proud of, one that would lead him to the heights of human experience.

When Leonard came around again, he stared at Tomas.

"It's OK," Tomas said, patting the air. "I'm not here to hurt you. I want to be friends. Do you know that word? 'Friends.'"

Leonard was uncertain of what to do next, but, after a few moments, he shuffled to the edge of the carousel and sniffed the air as if to test it.

Leonard revolved closer and Tomas got a clearer view of the extent of Leonard's deformities. The goiters and swellings. The patches of hair and scaly skin.

"It's OK," Tomas called, the carousel turning so Leonard was hidden again among the rods and wooden steeds. "I just want to be friends."

When Leonard returned, a distortion had overcome his frame, settling most startingly in his eyes.

There was no childlike innocence to them. Yellowed and sickly, they had more tiger than lamb. Tomas stood in their predatory focus and knew another pure experience as old as life. Fear. The fear mice have of hawks. The fear of lost calves at the howls in the night. There was no humanity in Leonard's eyes. Only an aggression so complex that Leonard's mind couldn't articulate it in anything but the hunched pose of a wild animal ready to pounce.

Like his laughter, Leonard's roar was hypnotic.

Tomas didn't react to Leonard climbing down his carousel and jettisoning toward him like a wounded ape. Only when Leonard was a few feet away, teeth bared and voice quaking, did Tomas turn to run. But his socks slid on the tile and he landed on his knees. Like a sugar-coated infant, Tomas crawled away as fast as he could.

Though nearly sprinting on all fours, Tomas knew it was useless—Leonard would tear him limb from limb—but the animal part of Tomas's brain strobed horrid scenarios at him, spurning him to be away, away, AWAY!

Something heavy landed on his back, flattening Tomas out and blasting the air from his lungs. His brain tried to summon all his strength and more. Only Tomas's arms responded, flailing fruitlessly. His legs had ceased to work. A big, grotesque paw clamped onto his back of Tomas's skull and pressed his forehead into the tile.

Screaming, Tomas felt the cheap tile crunch under his forehead and felt Leonard's weight on his neck. Behind his eyes, a pressure built until Tomas couldn't shut them against their swelling and forceful evacuation.

Blind, Tomas was consumed by the monstrous pressure. Yet, through it all, Leonard laughed, hearty and colossal, and the carousel continued to play its scratchy song.

—ETC.—

THE FLAMINGO OUT OF HIS CAGE

A galaxy of pain swallows everything up—the corner store, your full reusable grocery bag, the wine bottle you'd been reading. It hurts so bad you can hardly string together a coherent thought let alone understand the sudden harshness of this new reality.

You've never seen the driver before nor have you ever been in his car. Yet, there they are. He's large around the middle but his limbs are skinny like someone who rarely strains himself. His eyes contain a frantic sadness, an emotional weight which creases his face. He drinks your wine and uses his forearm to block the air rushing through the open maw of his shattered windshield.

"Man, I thought you hitchers were big talkers," he says, coughing and chuckling. "Alone most of the time, right? Damn, wine always get me craving a Small Mountain like a right-fucking-gentleman. No use with all this goddamn wind. Sorry, buddy, I don't know what happened to the windshield. I swear it was fine this morning. Must've been behind a big truck or something..."

Moving your eyes shows how broken you are and when you try to reach up and touch your face, nothing happens. Even the thoughts hurt your limbs... or what's left of them. Your right leg is gone at the knee and not by a surgeon's knife. One of your bloody arms is in view but it's so mangled there's no way to know if it's your right or your left.

You try turning your head but something in your neck cracks, sending an icy jolt through you. The sensation makes your body somehow even less responsive.

The inside of the car is chaos. Crushed glass has found every crease and fold—not just in the car but your clothes. A smear of blood on the dash connecting all the way to the dented hood. A piece of your sweater flutters wild on a stray snag. The driver doesn't seem to notice any of it.

"Well, stay quiet if you want," he says. "I appreciate a man who can keep secrets. Besides, I'm the one with the talking to do."

He turns the wine bottle upside down. When only dribbles touch his lips, he raises it above his waiting mouth to catch the drops, but the rushing air splatters wine up his nose. Coughing, he rolls his window down, throws out the bottle, and rolls it back up.

"I don't mean to speed, but don't worry. I know the roads," he goes on. "Plus, if you knew where I was headed, you'd say, 'Why, Frankie, my boy, you should've booked yourself a ticket on a rocket ship.' Oh-ho, if you only knew..."

"Help...," you groan—each vibration of your throat brings out tears—but your tongue if half gone and nothing really comes out.

"What's that? Can't hear you with—sorry about the windshield," he repeats. "I swear, it was fine—but that's how it's been going lately, I'll tell you." He rubs his eyes and looks at you. He sees but does not see. "The windshield, my dogs getting at my shoes"—he takes his foot off the accelerator to wiggle his naked toes at you—"but, man oh man, I'm on my way. *Wooo!*"

The noise jars you, slumping your body further down on the seat. The nub of your right leg presses into the crease between door and dashboard and stops you—the pressure makes your hip turn to fire. You're certain you've broken your pelvis.

"Got this lady waiting for me over at the Victoria Beer Garden," he says. "She was an old girlfriend from before I was married, when I was slim and strong and could fuck like a machine. All night, I tell you." He laughs and coughs. "Pass me a cigarette, would you? They're right there in the glovebox."

He points but doesn't wait.

"And this one, oh, she called me up last week and told me to come by—she owns it or part owns it, you know, one of those. Victoria Beer—It's got the arbors and—Anyway, you'll see it. I hope she hasn't changed, but you know women. Maybe she went the real *matronly* route, shut it down with a short haircut and thick jeans. But I don't know... She used to really take care of herself. Always in makeup, had a great little hardbody, and—you'll think I'm lying, but I ain't, buddy"—he knocks your knee playfully and you feel your bowels void—"had a twat that smelled like roses. Roses, I—oh, man, sorry. I know you guys can't shower and you're in the heat, but, good god, you stink!"

He pinches his nose, unaware of your blood on his knuckles. "You know, if we get a cigarette going—pass the Small Mountains. They're in the—oh, never mind—" He reaches over and opens the glovebox. The panel hits your leg and you whimper.

"What's that?" he shouts, arm whipping around in the dark glovebox. "You've got to speak up on account of the windshield," he reminds you. He finds the pack of Small Mountains and closes the glovebox.

Noticing he brushed your mangled leg, he apologizes, not knowing that though it's whole and bent at a weird angle, you can't feel any of it. "I ain't one of those," he assures you, putting his hand on your knee.

You nearly faint from the shock.

He pulls back a bloody hand and uses it to get a cigarette and light it. He tries a lighter at first, then remembers the wind and uses the car's push lighter instead. There are two red smudges on his lips from how he holds his cigarette. He blows the smoke out of his nose until he sneezes. The air sprays the snot across both your faces.

"So, she calls me up and—get this—she makes up some story about calling area customers about some concert that's going on tonight," he tells you. "And I hear her and hear the place and I say, 'Hey, isn't this Gabby Sedeno?' She says it is but real soft and innocent like she didn't know who she was calling."

He smokes and laughs.

Your broken body makes it so you can barely piece anything together. As he speaks, his words conjure an older woman into your mind. She could be your mother—or it might be your wife since you have no idea of the year or your age or anything about yourself. To you, now, pain is all you've ever known. The buildings in your mind could be home or work or a dream. There was no time before the agony a few miles ago.

"'Oh, c'mon, Gabby, don't pretend with me, it's Frank Fla- mingo' I told her," he says. "Oh-ho, you could almost smell it over the phone. 'Frankie? From school?' she says. 'Yeah, yeah. It's been a long time. We should get together, you know, rem- iniscence about the old days.' 'I dunno, Frankie, I'm real busy with the business especially with this concert,' she tells me. She hung up real quick, but she made me promise about the con- cert."

He finishes his cigarette, forcing the smoke out of the spaces between his teeth. He slaps around the car until he finds a dented beer can. Putting his knee against the bottom of the steering wheel, he opens it and takes two or three gulps. He smacks his lips and exhales big. "Oh, message received, Gabby. Message received," he says, giggling. "A woman like that, oh-ho, half the charm's in the chase... mostly because you know you're getting the catch."

You've given up on asking for help or trying to remember simple things like your age or your name. Dying would be best, you tell yourself, but you're too weak to even will yourself into the darkness.

"Oh-ho, we're getting close, my boy," he says, hitting the steering wheel.

Outside, it's the bright signs of gas stations and cheap restaurants. The car's deceleration and turns shift your organs. In your state, these changes feel permanent. The car slows. There are people—hobos and workmen and drunks and the na- ive—and while they all see the dented car with no windshield, it takes so long for them to notice you. When someone does, an old man of the street, he shouts something you can't understand.

Frankie hits the locks and drives away. The screams follow for a bit, but Frankie is moving too fast.

"Can you smell it?" He snuffles the air like a pig. Chuckling, he lights another cigarette with difficulty. "Roses, my friend, goddamn roses. And she's just the first of many. It was just a matter of time. The news just had to circulate that ol' Francis Gabriel Flamingo dropped the dead weight and is back on the market. It just had to get around and then that dumb cow will know all she did was set me free. Free to fuck, fuck—FUCK!"

He slams the brakes and you're thrown forward.

You can't stop the dashboard from rushing up to meet you nor how it flings you back against the seat again, your ribs and sternum sending painful zaps up and down your insides.

"We're here, buddy," he tells you, clapping you across the back.

You scream with such force something wet dislodges in your throat and slides down your windpipe, catching somewhere so it's like a thumb plugging a garden hose.

"Whoa, guy, I was going to say I've got wetnaps and mouthwash in the console," he tells you. "Get fresh and come in. But keep it straight. I'm hungry for it, you know—oh, nice, a spare," he said, finding another beat-up beer can. "They probably charge by the limb in here. That woman always was expensive."

He opens the beer, drinks it, and belches. He gets out of the car. The jostling movement helps clear your throat enough to grant you a few more agonizing minutes.

"And don't worry," he says, looking into the car. "Tell them you're with Francis Gabriel Flamingo. FLAMINGO. They'll unroll a red carpet for you. Eat, drink, be fucking merry, because tonight you're a king."

He shuts the door and walks toward an outdoor restaurant. There's a stage set up. A band plays a sad song and people smile and tap their feet. Above it all, you hear, "Watch out! The Flamingo's out the cage, people! *Wooo*!"

Frankie and the band fight for supremacy.

The music covers your soggy pleas. People trickle by. They point and laugh at the car, thinking the blood belongs to a deer or that, perhaps, it's paint. It isn't until a chubby couple comes by to take pictures of the damage that someone sees you. The woman screams so loud it puts a little life back in you. Her man calls for an ambulance.

It will not reach you in time. Just as there was no time before the driver and the pain, there's nothing after it either.

—ETC.—

THE HAUNTING OF FATHER DAVIES

I.

Sleeping pills made him loopy and even the mildest of tea played on the stomach of Father Davies something terrible so that all the next day he punctuated his sermons with rancid burps. The only sure thing that got Father Davies to sleep was reciting the "Our Father" or "Hail Mary" over and over. Even then, sometimes he'd be up all night repeating the prayers. But, that night, after reciting the "Our Father" sixty-seven times, the old priest managed to find some sleep.

Sometimes, during working hours, Father Davies stared at the people deep in prayer and wondered what gift heaven would grant them—love, respect, an existence without vice. Father Davies, though, desired nothing more than a good shit and full night's sleep.

In half-sleep, his conscious mind hovered over his pillow, dulling his scowl. He almost got there, but the phone ringing brought him back.

"Son of a bitch!" he cursed, then coughed up the loose phlegm produced by all the lying down. He answered the phone, shouting, "What in the hell's going on that you've got to call me in the middle of the damn night?"

"Father Davies?"

"Who the shit else would it be?"

"This is Dr. Norris from the county hospital," the voice said. "We've got a Catholic here in a bad way. I was told to get a hold of a priest for his last rites. Can you make it?"

The priest grumbled, saying, "Look at your clock. I ain't working until the morning. I'll be there then."

"Father," Dr. Norris implored. "The man won't make it that long. He requested you specifically before going under. You were his hometown priest it seems. I can't—"

"Someone from Dodd?" the priest asked, moving his legs off of bed. "Who?"

"His name is... Bulmaro Mejorado."

"Bulmaro... Bulmaro... Little Bully?" the priest said. "Almost thirty? Rail thin?"

"He was in a car accident—"

"Who's with him? His mother couldn't be—"

"A man named Zander Stone, his boyfriend," the doctor answered. "Father, I can't stress enough—"

"Still biting pillows, eh?" Davies asked.

"*Sir*! I don't—"

"You tell those queers the only man that ought to be inside them is Jesus!" the priest went on. "Tell them to pray! To get on their knees and really pray. That's what knees are for, not sucking each other off."

"The man is dying!"

"He died a little every time he looked at a man," Davies

continued. "Now, this better be the last time you call me in the middle of the night over some faggot. You can't save their souls, doctor. All I'd be doing is wasting the little breath I got left. God bless you and good night."

He slammed the phone down and worked his legs back into bed. Sleep, though, was no longer an option. Instead, he lay in the dark and thought about Bulmaro Mejorado, "Little Bully" around Dodd.

The boy had always been a little feminine, a little mincy, but Davies had known plenty like that who had a mess of children and faithful wives. There had even been a few of that type at the seminary. But in high school, Bulmaro came out to the town and was promptly exiled.

Thinking back on it, Father Davies was glad Dodd was still a God-fearing town. To pass the last hours of the night, Father Davies fell into childish fantasies and imagined himself a soldier in God's army, battling evil out on the Texas frontier. He could still keep his flock safe even as old as he was.

Near dawn, Davies considered offering up a prayer for Little Bully's soul—from what the doctor said, he wouldn't last the night—but he got up and made coffee instead. He poured himself a cup, mumbling, "You can't save what can't be saved."

II.

Father Davies saw the obituary in *The Daily Dodder* days later. The picture was from Bulmaro's high school graduation—he'd come out shortly after taking the photo and was all but tarred-and-feathered by the town. Sure, there'd been the liberals who took him in, who didn't spit on the sidewalk at the sight of him, but they weren't congregants. Those fools would burn one day with Little Bully and all his kind.

A week later, Father Davies felt the rumblings of a coffee-soaked bran muffin and shuffled to the toilet. He took the *Dodder* because it helped relax him and, in turn, his bowels.

On the front page was an article about a suicide who walked into one of the ICU rooms in the county hospital. There, he put a gun in his mouth and shot off the top of his skull. A note in his pocket said something to the effect that he'd lost the love of his life and that the world was cruel. He'd wanted to die where his lover had.

When the priest read the man's name, Zander Stone, he couldn't remember its significance. But, at the end of the article, in true small-town fashion, the reporter added that, "though unverified, sources say the deceased man was the sexual partner of former Dodd resident, Bulmaro Mejorado, who died last week after a collision on Highway 73."

The words made Father Davies's guts turn to iron, rigid and unmovable. He crumpled the paper in frustration, thinking, *Just like those queers, all drama and no substance. No endurance for the rules. Worst of all, he went and ruined probably the last good shit I had. Well, at least that's another one in the fire.*

Stomach still cramped, Father Davies pulled up his pants and flushed out of habit.

Satan worked as mysteriously as the Lord, Davies knew. Perhaps today, the Great Adversary had sacrificed two men to upset him, but Father Davies wouldn't be detoured. Lost souls already lost meant very little to him.

III.

The day was tiring but, for a man his age, all days were. For the priest, the world was a glorious ship that had struck something on its voyage and now sank slowly for the last forty years. Father Davies was forced to watch the world take on water. The good people drowned until they weren't human so much as talking sacks of sin and, no matter how many died or how many shamed family and community, the priest found more and more people were enticed to stray from the Lord.

The dying world weighed on him heavily that day. He hoped he'd be able to sleep, even just a few hours. He said his prayers in bed, knowing God wouldn't judge him for sparing his old knees from the unforgiving floor.

By the twentieth "Hail Mary," his frustration grew. He imagined the Holy Mother's serene and sorrowful face. More and more, Father Davies thought of that face whenever he passed fornicators or drunkards. Her face cooled his anger though it could never completely snuff it out.

The priest opened his eyes to the dark of the room.

A face hovered inches from his own. It was spectral, pale, disfigured. Though the eyelids were torn to shreds, the eyes were aflame with accusation.

Even with the burns and shredded cheeks, he recognized Bulmaro's face.

Davies tumbled out of bed, landing roughly on his side. He yelled in pain and tried to turn over to see how Bulmaro could be standing in his room, but the priest was alone.

He managed to reach the phone and call the local ambulance to collect him. After he told them what happened, the priest had to envision the Holy Mother again. Otherwise, he'd've taken a swing at the paramedics for saying it was just a nightmare.

IV.

The next day, Father Davies all but sprayed holy water on the rectory walls, shouting threats of divine retribution at cupboards and picture frames. Every doorway was sealed with water, which, once he was finished, made moving around treacherous. At his age, a simple stroll was walking a tightrope and his sling made him list to one side. He strafed the wall into his bedroom for safety's sake and said his prayers again.

His prayers weren't blessings but calls for vengeance. There were forces that wanted righteous souls and would stop at nothing to get them. Davies asked for Saint Michael's sword to keep the devils at bay so he could remain a loyal soldier of the Lord. He asked for God Himself to send cleansing flames across the foulness of the Earth because the world had been given choices and had chosen incorrectly. They no longer had the strength for morality, only depravity and sin.

After a while, the prayers stopped being coherent. From "Hail Mary, full of grace" to "those drugged up—no fathers and the schools are garbage—happy bearing drunk and—pregnant by twelve and all that" until the priest worked himself into a fit of coughing.

The coughs blew life into tiny embers in his throat. The sudden contractions jarred his injured arm so that he was wide awake. He held his arm for many minutes. Eventually, his heart slowed and his throat cooled. Father Davies wiped the tears of frustration from his eyes with his good hand.

When his eyes cleared, two figures floated above his bed.

The first was Bulmaro, still a catalogue of head wounds, while the other, chiseled and maintained even in death, was normal enough except when he smiled. His front teeth were bloody shards and, through them, the priest could see the ceiling.

The priest's age and sour disposition turned him fierce. "Away from me, Satan's sex toys! You've no power against an agent of the Lord God Almighty!" he declared, waving his fist. "You've no power to lay hands on me!"

"You're not really our type," Bulmaro said, his voice bubbling as though fighting its way through water.

"*I* could make an exception," the other teased, pursing his black-marked lips at Father Davies.

"Be gone strange creat—"

"Strange?" Bulmaro blurted, shaking his head in disbelief. His torn cheeks swayed like hung laundry. "You recognize me, don't you, Father? You have to. You baptized me, confirmed me, heard all my confessions and *still* I'm a stranger?"

"I know you're agents of Satan—"

"Hardly, Mr. Wrinkles," the second said, his dead eyes rolling.

"We're lost sheep left out in the cold," Bulmaro said. "By you."

"So, we had to keep warm," the second continued, his hands undoing Bulmaro's belt since, dead though he was, the pair were dressed for the grave. "I hope you enjoy the show."

The second pulled the spectral trousers down enough to reveal a translucent semi-erect cock. The second spirit took it in its hands and put his mouth onto it, pressing his face into Bulmaro's lap so far that the head of Bulmaro's cock peeked out of the gaping hole in the back of the spirit's skull.

The priest was disgusted. He tried to shimmy out of the bed, but his age and injuries made it impossible. And, moving his body uselessly back and forth, Davies was treated to the sight of the dead Bulmaro being devoured cockfirst.

"Don't worry, Father," Bulmaro huffed. "I'll be quick. Zander knows all my buttons."

The second, Zander, faced the priest. His mouth suddenly lost its solidity and Bulmaro's ghostly pecker speared his cheeks. "Not too soon. I'm going to give this old fart a cock sucking clinic," he promised.

Zander returned to his work with a renewed ferocity.

Father Davies was helpless through it all. He closed his eyes and prayed, but the volume of his thoughts couldn't drone out the wet sucking sounds.

V.

The phantasmagoric blowjob ended with ecto-ejaculate spraying out the back of Zander's head and into the air. When they were done, the two spirits were gone, yet the ectoplasmic semen remained, glowing and dissipating slowly into the atmosphere of the room.

The priest crossed himself and tried to pray, but each time he got going, he'd envision the sprayed ectoplasm. Two lines into an "Our Father," he'd think of the eagerness, the delight, with which Zander swallowed Bulmaro. Davies, shaking the image from his head, gave up on prayer soon after.

The process of getting out of bed was arduous. His arm stung as he balanced and stretched. Eventually, the priest got up and went into the rectory's kitchen to make coffee.

He sat and drank it with no pleasure. Looking around, he hated everything he saw. He'd been baptized in filth and sodomy, forced to endure what even repulsed God. Now, everything was distorted, the same in shape, sure, but the stains of sin were visible upon them.

The Daily Dodder sat on the edge of the table. He picked it up for distraction. SUICIDE VICTIM'S FAMILY STILL SEEKS ANSWERS, the headline read. Beneath it was a picture of a man who the priest recognized immediately, even without a hole in his head or a dick in his dead mouth.

VI.

At the morning service, Father Davies wanted to give a sermon about remaining vigilant and strong. There was a darkness that knew no virtue and it tried for their souls. Through minor sins uncorrected, through devotion left to wilt, even through sentimentality. As much as the Lord demanded that they venture to save souls, his congregants needed to tighten their ranks in preparation. Father Davies wanted to tell them he'd personally been visited by the minions of Hell... but that would put the images in his mind more than they already were.

In the middle of his sermon, Father Davies looked up at the stained glass above the main doors. Christ, hardly clothed, and the two flanking thieves, whose faces flashed with ethereal shapes, sending his mind back to the macabre fellatio the night before.

Any hope of a meaningful sermon was gone.

Father Davies hurried through the rest of the mass and went to the rectory to eat something that could, hopefully, get his rusty bowels moving.

VII.

Not all the prune juice nor fiber pills in Dodd could get more than a fart out of him. All he did on the toilet was nod off. After hours, the priest got up, low back aching, and lifted his pants, an action so painful, he could only bend an inch at a time. Father Davies just stood in the bathroom catching his breath once he was finished.

He opened the mirrored medicine cabinet and got a bottle of aspirin. Too stiff to walk to the kitchen, Davies took the pills with palmfuls of faucet water.

In his room, he sat on the single chair and opened his bible. The feel of the crinkled pages alone put him at ease. But that day, with intestines like a chained-up dog and brain nearly mush from lack of sleep, the pages comforted him very little.

He decided to pray instead, but his mind couldn't hold onto anything. A "Hail Mary" almost finished turned into "The Act of Contrition" before closing as "The Declaration of Faith." The fragmented prayers grew into a familiar frustration. But it was in that frustration that Father Davies looked down at the bible in his lap.

"Finally, be strong in the Lord and in His mighty power," the pages read. "Put on the full armor of God so that you can take your stand against the devil's schemes. For our struggle is not against flesh and blood, but against the rules, against the authorities, against the powers of this dark world and against the spiritual forces of evil in the heavenly realms."

Father Davies reread the words again and again, each pass igniting the fire in him, a weathered soldier of the Lord. He had the belt of truth firmly on and the breastplate of righteousness armored his body. But, reading as he did, most importantly, the old priest realized he still had the sword of the Spirit because it was the holy Word which Davies could recite faster than any witch could open a spell book of deviltry.

He got up and began his preparations for war. The ease of his movements was the grace of God that healed him for the upcoming battle... or the aspirin kicked in.

VIII.

The pot of coffee and lack of sleep made Father Davies jittery and woozy all at once. Dressed in his finest vestments and holy relics—pieces of hair and shreds of death shrouds removed from dead saints—and an ornate rosary, Father Davies waited in bed. He held his bible and a simple wooden crucifix.

By three in the morning, the repetitive thought of spiritual warfare grew stale and the only remaining effect the coffee had was a full bladder. Still, the priest didn't move. The enemy, he knew, would strike when he was most vulnerable. They were cowards. The moment he worked his pants down, they'd attack with all their queer fury. They'd waited until he was feeble, but he'd show them through grit and a disciplined bladder and on their fiery fall back to Hell, they'd know they sure fucked with the wrong one.

At four, he realized he'd piss himself if he waited any longer. He couldn't have that. The cleaning woman would see it. Word would make its way up to the bishop and then Davies would be forcibly retired. The priest made quick work of pissing—no more than ten minutes—but, on his return, he heard voices in his bedroom.

He opened the door and found the gay phantoms embraced in spectral nudity. Davies took the bible from between his arm and ribs.

"If we fuck on the bed, do you think he'll sleep on the floor like a dog?" Zander asked, burying his face into the skin flaps of Bulmaro's cheeks.

"Be gone, devils!" Father Davies shouted, waving his bible. "By the will of the one true God, you will face divine retribution. By the Sacred Blood of Christ, I command you! Leave the realm of men! Be exiled to your judgment. Let God have sight of you so you may know true fear! By the power of God, I cast you out—"

As Davies thundered, Bulmaro had floated around Zander and entered the suicide from behind. There was no look of pleasure on Bulmaro's maimed face, though. Father Davies thought he saw vexation.

Spurred on by Bulmaro's expression, the priest continued, "Cast the souls of these two fornicators back into the fires! It is by the Word you are damned!"

Bulmaro pushed himself deeper into Zander until his phantom cock poked out of the prostrated ghost's mouth like a third eye. "You don't get it, you old bitch? It's by the Word we're here."

"It's the devil's—"

The skewered ghost moved forward, dislodging the cock from his throat, and said, "*He* told us—and not with some dusty old book, but *told* us—He was tired of a bunch of old idiots getting the message mixed up with the words and wanted to make amends for all the shit people like you put us through. He believes in justice. The real kind."

"So, here we are," Bulmaro said, gyrating faster behind his partner. "And here we'll be... because He listens, Father. Even if I wasn't balls-deep in asshole, giving you the news would get me stiff. He listens. All you want, all you really pray for now, is sleep and a nice shit... Father, you're never sleeping again and the best shit you'll have won't fill a thimble."

Zander smiled, his broken teeth naked to the light, and said, "We've got eternity, Father. But you don't. So, relax. You might even start enjoying it." Zander opened his mouth like a cannon.

The priest was silent as a snowstorm of ectoplasmic semen spewed from Zander's mouth and filled the room.

IX.

Father Davies's decline was rapid. His masses were shorter, his sermons slurred, each ending with blank stares at the church doors. Once he even drooled into his open prayer book.

The priest ate close to nothing except Maverick Market laxatives. He ate them on the spot and, usually, fell asleep on the customer toilet until someone unlocked the door and got him. More and more, he told people they were queers and fornicators. Even to Sister Agnes he said, "Fuck off, you rug-munching dozer!"

When agents of the diocese were called for a site evaluation, he let them into the rectory and asked where his fellow priests planned to disrobe and lube up before he doused them in bottles of holy water.

When the county was called to collect him and ship him off to the Almeida psych-ward nearby, Father Davies did not go quietly. He bit and spat and yelled. He was a soldier of God in need of a hearty battalion full of guts and vigor and good old-fashioned heterosexuality, he said to anyone who'd listen.

By the next Sunday, a replacement had been found. The church bells rang as loud as before and, at noon, the people gathered at the church doors same as ever. More than a few offered prayers for Father Davies, their old priest, thinking he was at the end of his life.

None knew he was in a small room, fretfully shouting against his medically induced sleep, kept alive by a competent staff and copious amounts of drugs. "You brainless heathens," he'd say, "once I nod off, they'll start cock-stabbing each other and you'll never get the juices off the walls let alone off your goddamn souls!"

—ETC.—

WE SELL PICKLES

for Simbry

I.

Fritz swept dust into a plastic dustpan and threw it into the trash. But, even old and from a distance, Peepaw saw the line of dirt left over.

The boy was agitated and it made him sweep absolutely for shit. Not that the shop had to look all that neat. People didn't come for the cement floors or the white-washed walls but for Peepaw's famed pickles. They drove hundreds—sometimes thousands—of miles and handed over wads of cash for jars of the stuff.

"Fritz, go ahead and sweep that again," Peepaw said from his leaning-spot in the corner. Peepaw, himself, resembled the pickles he sold. He was a short man of few dimensions and had a distinct bump on the side of his nose. "And, thinking on it, after, go straighten out those jars over there. Line those labels up uniform-like, like I tell you."

Fritz threw his head back, his shoulders dropping as though the broom and dustpan suddenly weighed a tremendous amount. He gave a pained look to the clock on the wall.

"Not the clock," the elder said, pointing. "The spot where you just were."

"Peepaw," Fritz complained. "It's two minutes to five. Let's just lock up."

"I wasn't aware I was keeping you from something," Peepaw said. "Got somewhere to be?"

"Uh... well..."

"Hey! Remember, I'm the one doing your mom the favor," he told Fritz. "She doesn't want you snorting your this or smoking your that. It's not like I need someone to sweep the floors like crap. I did that fine before—"

"It's just... I told Alexandra I'd meet her after work," Fritz confessed. "She's going to wait for me on the bench outside the candy shop. I promised I'd bring a jar of spicy garlic—"

"Stay away from that girl," the elder snapped. "It's the pickles she wants... And not the one you're trying to give."

Fritz's face slumped. "Not everyone's after our pickles."

"*My* pickles. And, yes, they are."

"No, Peepaw, they're—"

"A two-hundred-year-old recipe and you think—Everyone's after these pickles. It's all they talk to me about."

Fritz groaned. "That's because you never leave the store."

Peepaw grinned. "You got me there. We close when we close, so get sweeping."

II.

Councilman Taylor had no idea how many bottles of cola he'd had. He'd hardly moved from his bench for hours. He watched the pickle shop with a quiet disdain. WE SELL PICKLES was written on the lone sign in the window and, to Taylor's annoyance, the county records showed the shop was registered as simply PICKLES. During his stakeout, he counted over a hundred people going in with money and coming out with armfuls of pickle jars. Thinking of all that money really bothered the councilman.

As head of Dodd's Chamber of Commerce, Taylor looked at their little downtown as a point of pride. Dodd, itself, was an agriculture town dominated by a big slaughterhouse so the old-time architecture and painted block of storefronts on Main was a bit of refinement... except for the eyesore WE SELL PICKLES. Unlike the other shops, WE SELL PICKLES bore no decorations, even during christmas or easter when all of downtown gussied themselves up with bunting and ribbons and window paint.

Even worse, the store sat near one of the first corners of downtown so that the diminutive—and creatively compliant—Cheryl's Honey Haus was dwarfed by the big windows and uniformed rows of pickles, onions, okra, jalapeños, and anything else that could be pickled, all beneath a paper sign declaring WE SELL PICKLES in black marker.

Sure, WE SELL PICKLES may have only turned away a handful of people a week, but Dodd could use every penny after the bad press because of those silly murders.

On the sly, offers were made to replace WE SELL PICKLES. Everything from cafes, antique shops, a locally sourced wine room, and two leather companies offered to have Peepaw Pickle's legs broken to move any deal along. Yet, dislodging WE SELL PICKLES, Taylor found, was nearly impossible.

Not only did the old pickle man pay his rent on time—in full—he did so months in advance. Of all the shop owners, he alone never complained about the county appraisal that raised their rent. And, worse still, people loved those pickles.

Everyone Taylor saw go into the shop came out carrying jars and smiling. They came from all over too. Taylor took special notice of the out-of-state plates and, the further the state, the more they'd park on the street and walk right past the other shops and their nice displays to go right into WE SELL PICK-LES. These out-of-towners usually left the shop with sloshing pickle jars and expressions that reminded Taylor of an uncle of his who used to huff antifreeze. Some pickle eaters even drove off with a pickle sticking out from between their teeth like cigars.

Sipping his soda, Taylor went over his plan. Past closing, he'd break into WE SELL PICKLES. Surely, there'd be something he could find—a violation or evidence of a crime—to finally be rid of the pickle store. Often, he'd seen Peepaw Pickle spit his chew on the street and, Taylor was certain, he probably did so around the pickles.

It was good for Taylor that Peepaw Pickle was as rigid with his schedule as he was with his lack of community participation.

III.

Councilman Taylor wasn't sure how so much grass could grow between buildings when the alleys hardly got any light but, as the sun set, he found himself in thigh-high grass behind the strip of downtown stores. Taylor waited until the last few minutes of light before prying open the WE SELL PICKLES service door with a small crowbar. The door made a loud, painful sound.

Before slipping into the building, Taylor waited a few moments to see if anyone heard. He entered a service space meant for electricians and plumbers to do their routine checks away from any customers and tourists. Those spaces doubled as emergency exits for shopkeepers who might be in back during a fire or some other emergency.

Taylor knew enough to disconnect the fire door so he wouldn't set off the alarm. If it went off, the county fire department would swarm en masse because the fire department often had very little to do around Dodd.

The backroom was long and wide with barrels of cucumbers and okra and peppers lined up against the walls. A big worktable in the middle was stained from the splashes of pickle juice and vegetable debris. The vinegar smell made Taylor dizzy.

Still, he clapped and readied his disposable camera. After running his finger across the surface of the table, he cursed. There was nothing on his finger. Not so much as a smudge of residue. The table, he was shocked to find, wasn't even sticky.

The jars, Taylor prayed, had to be dirty. But, like the table, they gleamed pristine in the camera flash. He doubted a single one would even photograph cloudy.

Next were the barrels. But, for those, Taylor planned to snot in them and scratch his head until the surface got a light dusting of graying hair. Yet, he hadn't anticipated the smell.

He'd almost gotten used to the vinegar smell seeping from the hundreds of pickle jars, but opening a barrel, Taylor made the mistake of inhaling deeply. The garlic and vinegar and capers singed the inside of his nose, clinging to the sensitive flesh. Crashing through the place, he coughed until his eyes watered. The only thing to bring him out of it was a doorknob jamming him painfully in the hip.

He hissed—ingesting more sharp pickled air—and used his tie to cover his nose and mouth. Catching his breath, Taylor saw a door, nearly hidden, in the dim depths of the room. It bore a paper sign that read NO ENTRY! ESPECIALLY YOU, FRITZ!

Taylor's imagination ran with all the possibilities of what lay behind the door. A hidden trash pile, a stash of at-home bugspray stored in non-government-approved ways, maybe a whole stack of crates filled with rotten cucumbers that Peepaw Pickle sold to save money. Whatever was hidden behind the door, there were possibilities while, in the current room, there was just antiseptic frustration.

The door was locked, but the doorframe was so warped that the latch was exposed. Taylor used his councilman's ID to open it. There was no trash, no fetid crates. Instead, there was a narrow staircase going down into darkness.

Taylor was stunned. There were no basements on that block, least of all any that looked to stretch below the neighboring stores. He found a light switch that cast the stairs in a dull yellow and descended the steps. The stairs ended almost fifteen feet below street-level and emptied into a hall of brick, its floor plain cement.

To his right, the hall dead-ended at a set of heavy wooden shelves laden with cloudy pickle jars. To his left, the hall stretched another fifteen feet or so, ending with a wooden door.

The door looked almost as old as the town. Iron bands kept the planks together and light glowed between the slats.

Taylor found that door unlocked.

IV.

The door revealed a gigantic glass vat of pickle juice braced with iron reinforcements of an ancient make. Vegetable scraps and spices swirled slow in the sickly yellow-green solution. The walls surrounding the vat were covered in framed pictures and articles about WE SELL PICKLES. Among them as well was an outdated pinup calendar.

Taylor looked at the vat and imagined Peepaw Pickle filling it with premeasured ingredients so it might taste good enough to blight downtown Dodd for another decade. Taylor smiled, thinking if the pickle man went to such effort to conceal the vat, it must be his most precious secret. Yes, there were plenty of vendors who'd love to know Peepaw Pickle's recipes. Taylor imagined that with some well-groomed competition, WE SELL PICKLES might be outclassed into closing.

Taylor looked around for something to collect the pickle juice but there was nothing but a filthy bucket and if anyone was to mimic the pickle brine, the sample had to be clean. Relatively.

He found a dusty jar out in the hall. The *pop* of its unsealing was like a gunshot. Shaking his furrowed nose at the closed stink in the jar, Taylor blew into it, sending a nimbus of dust into his own face. Back at the vat, he looked for some kind of spigot or valve but couldn't find one. Exhausting all options on the ground, Taylor looked up at the vat's heavy lid.

Sighing, he reminded himself that a little trouble now would grant Dodd a future without WE SELL PICKLES and when Taylor, an old man, would look at Dodd's beautiful, quaint downtown on some distant holiday, there'd be solid blocks of festive decorations and shopkeepers that understood the value of a cohesive community. Dreaming of some distant christmas, Taylor went and found a stepladder to get him up to the lid.

Taylor found the lid and its wheel-latch were in good working order, dusted and oiled. Taylor couldn't think of a place to put the jar, so he stuck it between his thighs and tried opening the lid. The wheel groaned with each turn and, finally, the lid shook as it released. The lid was heavy and when Taylor pushed it open the stepladder clattered on its legs. The lid, swung up on its hinges, landed with a resounding crash that nearly knocked Taylor off the stepladder. Balance regained, he checked the glass sides for cracks.

Seeing no leaks, Taylor steadied himself. One jar and they're gone, he thought, dipping the jar achilles-like into the pickle juice. It filled a little but, seeing shreds of vegetable-matter, Taylor leaned further, scooping them into the jar. It was best to get as many ingredients as possible. Taylor swirled the juice around in hopes of corralling more of the brine stuff.

There was what looked like the bulb of a small dark-rooted onion and Taylor went after it like it was a prize. He had to get on his tiptoes, but he got it.

"Success," he whispered, bringing the jar up so he could look at his find. It swirled and tumbled and somersaulted to reveal itself with such a startling clarity that Taylor forgot to breathe. Turning gracefully in the jar was a human eye. Slightly shriveled, the whites dyed the sickly green-yellow of pickle brine, the root hardly more than black threads.

Taylor dropped the jar into the vat, not thinking of retrieving it. He had to get the sheriff. He'd thought to catch WE SELL PICKLES violating health codes not hiding body parts.

But, as he descended the rickety stepladder, something like a shadow within the depths of the vat caught his eye.

The shape rising and breaking the brine's surface caused a vinegar eruption. It lay across the lip on its side like a newly beached whale.

The pickled thing had once been a man. An old one. His body had shrunk and wrinkled like a drowned thumb. The hands were curled up near its bearded chin. Within one eye was a thick garlic clove brined the same yellow as the pickled thing's horrid teeth.

Taylor took a moment to get the courage to examine the body. He reached to touch it. The slick skin repulsed him and he took a step down. He needed to be away and far from WE SELL PICKLES, he thought. But the pickled thing wanted something different.

It snatched at Taylor's arm and tried to pull itself out of the vat. It exhaled in bursts, each word a sharp spell that splattered herbs and vegetable bits across Taylor's face. It cleared its throat by gurgles and coughs and slapped around until he felt Taylor. The pickled thing clutched Taylor's arms with an unreal strength. Its old mouth, grey-gummed and sparsely toothed, enveloped Taylor's hand. The leathery tongue wriggled all through Taylor's fingers.

The pickled thing retched. "Terrible! Terrible! They're goddamn terrible!" it spat. "Those are the worst damn pickles I ever tasted, you dumb little shit! My pecker spitting out a no-good know-nothing like you is god's cruel joke, I'll tell you."

Taylor shrieked and lost his footing. His hand, greased with spit, slid from the pickled thing's grasp. In his fall, Taylor caught the lip of the vat but that only gave the pickled thing a chance to slap around and catch the councilman again.

"They ain't got no spice," it said, his wooden fingers digging into Taylor's forearms. "They ain't got no snap. They're all soft and pudgy like a fat lady's fingers."

The pickled thing couldn't hold Taylor who fell to the ground. One of the pickled thing's hands and most of its other arm were locked onto Taylor's sleeve and wouldn't let go. The bones popped from their sockets and the soggy flesh tore like cheese cloth and the arm landed alongside Taylor on the floor.

Yet, the pickled thing still clung onto the lip of the container, the juice churning from its wild kicking. "Ain't much left in this jar but me and the recipe, you lout, and I ain't ever writing it down. Not now, not never!" it rambled, yammering vaguely about recipes and whoresons and dill-spiced legacy. "They promised me sons for my pickles and gave me nothing but bums—BUMS!—I swear by this brine—"

Taylor didn't stay to hear the rest.

As fast as his portly body allowed, he limped through the cellar hall and to the foot of the steps, all the time looking behind him and fearing that the pickled thing had gotten out of its container and belly-crawled after him.

But the pickled thing was content howling in its vat. Relieved, Taylor took the first step up the stairs but stopped.

Peepaw Pickle and his grandson stood at the top of the stairs.

"Well, Fritz," the old man said. "Looks like we've got ourselves a real dilly of a pickle, don't we?"

"Sure do, Peepaw. We sure do."

V.

"—and that's why you're going down there and cleaning his tank," Peepaw said, loading a heavy box into the back of his truck.

Glum-faced, Fritz crossed the sidewalk into the store and got another box from a tall stack. When he returned, he handed Peepaw the box, saying, "He doesn't like me and he's weird—"

"Watch it, boy!" Peepaw snapped. "That's my great-great-grand-peepaw and no shit he's weird. He's two hundred years old and being blind and pickled ain't doing his brains any favors. So, you'll go down there and treat him with respect. He's fed us for generations."

"I don't know why I have to—"

"Because it's your fault," Peepaw said. "You're always out back smoking your stuff. And don't think I don't smell it on account of the pickles neither because I do."

Fritz groaned, beginning an excuse, and a box slipped from his grasp. It hit the sidewalk and the glass inside clinked together. Both heard a muffled crunch.

Peepaw sighed. "And you wonder why you annoy the man. He spends his day in a jar and gets to come out to a careless no-good—"

Fritz crouched and prodded the box with his fist. "I think it's OK."

Peepaw was struck dumb. "You think... You what? Go ahead. Pick it up. Go on."

Fritz lifted the box—its contents crunched and clinked— and took it over to Peepaw.

The old man cut the tape seal with a pocketknife. He opened it, showing the contents to Fritz, and said, "They look 'OK'?"

The late evening painted everything in shadow, but the contents were undeniable. A jar filled with garlic and dill and peppers broken. Pickles strewn all over though not in enough abundance to hide the pieces of Taylor. A plump hand. An ear. An eye and tongue.

"I swear," Peepaw said. "Drop another and I'll put you in the vat to keep him company, you—"

"Y'all ain't usually open this late," a voice called. "Trouble with the help?"

Peepaw and Fritz turned.

Sheriff Leiben shut his cruiser door and walked up to them.

Raising his hand to acknowledge the lawman, Peepaw chuckled and said, "I think I'm madder at myself for expecting more out of a lousy teenager."

"Don't be too hard on him," the sheriff said, shaking Peepaw's hand. Then he saw the leaking box in Fritz's arms. "Oh! Wasting good pickles, huh?" The sheriff shook his head. "That's a hanging offense in Dodd, son." The sheriff smiled. "But... for a box of pickles"—he pointed to the stack near the door—"I'm sure I can look the other way."

"You don't want them pickles," Peepaw said. "The boy here put water in the brine instead of vinegar and ruined enough product to have him as slave labor until he's a man."

Peepaw snapped his fingers. "Get the sheriff four of the garlic and four of the... The missus likes okra, right?"

The sheriff nodded.

"Four of the okra. Mild?"

"You know she's got the ulcer..."

"Mild," Peepaw concluded, waving Fritz away.

Peepaw and the sheriff spoke about the heat while Fritz filled a box with jars of pickles and okra. The sheriff didn't take a step before opening the box and retrieving a jar. He selected a small pickle and ate it in two bites. In a satisfied daze, the sheriff got in his cruiser and left. He waved to them with another pickle in his hand.

Peepaw and Fritz waved back until the sheriff was gone.

"Hurry up with those boxes," Peepaw told him. "Break another and you'll be cleaning the tank with your toothbrush."

–ETC.–

ABSTINENCE! ABSTINENCE!

I.

All day Father Milagro felt squirrelly. It was an even, sunny day with the right amount of wind—enough to cool the city but not enough to get his allergies going. His coffee was the perfect color and his dullest parishioners had stayed home. All in all, his day's little uppers put an idea in his head.

When it came time for his sermon, Father Milagro abandoned his discussion of John the Baptist and the whole head chopping thing. Instead, he wanted to talk about a book he'd finished the day before.

"Dante's *Inferno*," he began. "You know, a man walks through Hell to find salvation."

Father Milagro was in his fifties and decades of pan dulce gave him enough belly to rest his hands on when he walked.

"I know you're thinking, 'Why-oh-why is the padre reading books about Hell?' Isn't the big one enough? Well, you got to know it to stay out of it, right? See the thing about the *Inferno* is what happens to all those the sinners. It's called a contrapasso. Now, I didn't know that—it was a footnote in the dollar-copy I bought—but it means that what we do here, now, that's coming back to get you."

Father Milagro walked off the altar place and strode along the front pews. "Say, for example, you were greedy. Then you'll have to carry bags of gold across a lake of fire so vast the sun'll go dark before you hit the first leg. Say you're a gossip, maybe you'll need help and, for once, no one's interested in what you're saying.

"But the real point of it is this," he said, returning to the pulpit. "When we're forced to lay our sins out in front of God, it doesn't matter the excuses. Cite every good deed if you want but on that day you'll remember every time you told me my sermons were great just to spare my feelings even though you were daydreaming about football."

The priest paused for a laugh that never came.

"Either way, when judgment is passed, we won't be anything more than the sum of our sins. You won't be the man who gives to the sheriff's toy drive or the woman who donates every time the blood van comes along. You'll just be greed. Or vanity. Or lust. That's it."

Usually, Father Milagro wouldn't've brought up lust during the sermon because of the impressionable children in attendance, but it was a squirrelly day and, as such, he let the big words fly.

"So, remember," he concluded. "Sure, *we* can't see our sins. That's our blessing. But your sins stick to you. Unless you truly repent—"

As he spoke, a horrendous stench and the sound of splashing water filled the church. The commotion came from the closed church doors. Liquid filth squirted through the spaces in the doors enough to make puddles in the foyer. Suddenly, the doors swung open and in rolled a living wave of muck and filth.

The entire congregation watched in fascinated terror as the muck moved down the aisle. It retained its borders like a loose gelatin-mold. Once completely in the church, then the people's brains registered the stink of seemingly every septic tank in the city boiled over like unattended moose soup. They vomited as they scattered and the living slick collected itself at the altar steps.

Soaking up the congregants' vomit, the living muck expanded like a balloon until it was nearly six feet tall. It became cloudy and translucent. Amidst the expanding filth, a cluster of waste floated to the surface. Though Father Milagro couldn't see clearly, he felt the nucleus of waste scrutinizing him.

Beneath it, a toothless mouth formed. The words sounded like they were spoken through a busted intercom underwater. "Creator?" it asked.

Father Milagro stifled a gag against the rank smell of its breath. "God is all of our—"

"No," it said. "*You.*"

From within its innards, the living muck produced a handkerchief kept it in a plastic bag for preservation. It held it out so the priest could clearly see the name embroidered on it. Milagro Canseco.

II.

It was a proud day for not-quite-Father Milagro. He and ten others were to give their vows and be welcomed as agents of God. Heaven's sublimity would flow through them when the overseeing cardinal for the San Ignacio de Junio Divinity School granted them the powers to, among other things, hear confession, to baptize, and to transubstantiate.

His mother and brother were in attendance. They waited to watch him walk up to the altar in all his finery. Waiting in a side hallway for the ceremony to begin, Milagro fiddled with his mother's gift. It was an ornate handkerchief with his name embroidered on its edge. His mother bought him one because she noticed priests used handkerchiefs to clean out the chalice at the end of mass.

The shuffle of twenty small sets of feet brought his focus into the hall.

Tours for the local Catholic school prayer clubs were often arranged and the seminary was big enough to host them during the ceremony. The children, no more than twelve years old, were all bored. Sorry this pivotal moment in his life wasn't more exciting for them, Milagro smiled.

He almost slipped back to thoughts of his family when *she* walked in. He'd never know her name—he took to remembering her as Julia, the name of a neighbor girl of his youth who resembled her.

She was beautiful, her ochre skin striking beneath a thick mane of dark brown hair. Her loose slacks still showed the curve of her hips. She wore a hauntingly tight sweater that clung to her heavy breasts. There was no denying them no matter how she tried.

One last temptation before a lifetime of celibacy, Milagro thought.

She approached the line of soon-to-be priests with the bored children trailing and congratulated them. A few shook hands with the children, one asked Julia a lot of questions, and Milagro just watched. The way her lips pulled back to smile, how she tucked her hair behind her unadorned ears. Her chest rose and fell like a love song as she made small talk.

For an instant, Milagro entertained a fantasy as deep and intricate as a lifetime. Julia straddled him in their small apartment while his face was smothered by her perfect breasts. He imagined through the eye of God, watching that sinful moment with passive indifference. Milagro imagined kissing her with the sunrise and whispering, "Good morning, Julia," before falling back into sin. The fantasy was gone as quickly as it appeared.

His erection, though, grew slowly and steadily. Milagro tried to fight it by holding his breath—a middle school trick—and imagined Brother Johannes, the seminary's obese chef, who often walked naked through the locker rooms with a towel slung over his shoulder. Neither trick worked.

Under his breath, Milagro prayed the machines within would cease functioning but realized it was pointless to ask God when, in a way, it was Milagro's own fault—planning for his vows, he abstained from touching himself for weeks. Just the night before, feeling anxious, Milagro almost gave in, but, after reciting the word "abstinence" like a prayer, he went to sleep.

At that moment, though, all he could think of was reliev-ing himself. Looking at his watch and feeling he wasn't going to soften anytime soon, Milagro knew there were no options.

He reached into the pockets of his cassock, grabbed a hold of himself, and pressed his erection against his hip. Pretending he'd forgotten something, Milagro excused himself, not that his fellow soon-to-bes paid him any attention with Julia around.

There was a bathroom upstairs seldom used since it was favored by Brother Balthazar, the organist, known for his pun-gently poor digestion. Though Brother Balthazar often prom-ised to eat more fiber, his digestive moans went through the seminary like poltergeists. But Milagro didn't need comfort, just solitude.

Once upstairs behind the locked bathroom door, Milagro was struck by a specter of shit stink. It was tolerable enough for what promised to be short work. The way he felt, Milagro thought, he wouldn't need more than four strokes.

His erection was intense and the sensations emanat-ing from it were undeniable. His fantasy picked up where it stopped. The thought of her breasts, her smell, the feel of her hair hanging over him was enough to move him closer to finish-ing. But, as he felt the early-warnings of an orgasm, he sucked in a deep breath of air and smelled the lingering stink of Broth-er Balthazar and the fantasy pulled away like a racing car.

Frantically, futilely, Milagro tried to grab at it as it rushed away—he got no softer but the feeling in his shaft was numbing so the process was exhausting, like sharpening a knife—and in-stead, Milagro had to replace all the greatest masturbation hits with Julia to continue. His thoughts went from mild to wild to kink. At first, Julia praised him, telling him he was a real cool guy, yet, in an instant, he demanded to put his face between her thighs—in his mind, he demanded it, "Right now, right now, right now, RIGHT NOW!" And then he was begging her to piss on him, to beat him, and when she said YES, Milagro came and took the Lord's name in vain as he did it.

There was only a square of toilet paper and, worrying he might soil his black cassock, Milagro caught the load in his hand.

Catching his breath, he looked at his watch. The ceremony was set to begin in ten minutes. He went to the sink. There was no soap, but Milagro would've been happy with plain water. Milagro opened the faucet and got nothing but the distant groan of empty pipes.

Panic set in. He pulled the handkerchief from his pocket and wiped his hand before he realized what he'd done. Disgusted in himself, Milagro unfurled the semen-splattered rag. He thought of his family outside, thought of God in the very air around him, and thought of how God's judgement would be terrible for sinners like Milagro.

He threw the handkerchief into the toilet and flushed it.

He watched his shame spin in the toilet... then stop. The water rose with his handkerchief on top.

At that moment, Milagro prayed like never before that if God would just flush his shame away, he'd always try to be a good man and a mouthpiece for God's will. The water receded after a few "Our Fathers" and Milagro went on to take his vows and go twenty years thinking that was the end of that.

III.

Father Milagro stared at the preserved handkerchief in disbelief. The mass of sentient sewage allowed him time to digest the information. When he was finally able, Milagro looked at his gelatinous child, settling eventually on the clump of plastics and unknown trash scraps he figured was its face. "How...," he said, but his son's loud, burbling voice was first.

"I am Ponzu," it said. "I don't recall the moment of my birth. I simply was. One moment nothing. The next, the sewers... Where you banished me. I lived like a beast—no!—*worse* than a beast. At least animals can seek companionship. But there are no others, Father? Agreed?" Venom was evident even with the burbling.

When it shouted, Ponzu stretched and thinned. "No, *I* was driven by hunger! Endless days of lurking after any movement, seizing anything alive—"

Suddenly, retreating, Father Milagro saw bits of bones—animal, human—among Ponzu's nucleus.

"—eating and eating until I'd finally eaten enough," Ponzu went on. "Until one day I became *aware*. I had half a drowned child digesting in me when I had my first thought: Why? I wanted to know why I was surrounded by piss and shit and rats and *fucking* rot! Why? What had I ever done to be cursed to the dark?"

A ripple went through Ponzu. "I learned from the trash. I learned to read. My name comes from the first word I learned to read off a bottle. Many letters later, I read the name of my creator. You. Milagro Canseco. He who gave me life. He who made my first days nothing but terror and confusion. Not even left to die because, to you, I never lived! My birth-pipes led to 2395 Wagner, the seminary, but there was no one there. After much searching, now I've found you."

"I don't know what—what can I do—" Father Milagro stammered, mystified.

Ponzu's liquid sneer bubbled and softened. Its body, too, shrank. Two sludge arms emerged like angel's wings. "Just give your baby boy a hug already," Ponzu cried, enveloping the priest.

Father Milagro, overpowered by the stink of raw sewage, vomited, only adding to Ponzu's form. Retching, Milagro felt the amorphous Ponzu embrace him tighter. He held his breath, found Ponzu's nucleus, and embraced it as best as he could.

IV.

It was only when Milagro was getting eyedrops at the pharmacy—his conjunctivitis would've blinded Paul all over again—and finally away from Ponzu's miasma that he understood the gravity of his mistake. He blamed his trance on Ponzu's smell because keeping his stomach from diving out his throat made Milagro easily influenced. Otherwise, there was no way the priest would've agreed to their new living arrangement. Instead of casting Ponzu out or calling on God to smite the foul creature, he'd invited Ponzu into the townhouse the church provided him.

Ponzu immediately stained everything.

He splashed the walls, soaked the rug, and ruined the couch within minutes. Within a few days, an HOA agent informed Father Milagro of the numerous complaints, all but one of them for a horrible stench. The other was for a missing cat, one known to frequent Father Milagro's small yard. The priest feigned ignorance on its fate, though he was sure Ponzu's nucleus now had a small collar in it.

Had it only been neighborhood alienation or a touch of feline homicide, Milagro may have resigned himself to it. But with clear sinuses came a clearer memory of the previous night's conversation.

Ponzu had called Father Milagro to the kitchen table—not even donation worthy now after being water-logged by living sewage—and said, "I've heard enough shrieks to know what I look like."

Father Milagro tried to put his hand over Ponzu's arm but it sank through it. He pulled back slimy threads of muck.

"Yet, I see that though I look like this," Ponzu continued, "I have humanity in me. I am not satisfied. I thought I only wanted to know you. That would've been enough, I hoped. To know... But... I fear that if all I've come for is *this*—and nothing else—I've made a mistake."

Father Milagro hadn't understood.

"I have found you," Ponzu told the priest. "But to what end? To know the sound of your voice, the lines of your face and... What? Go back to the mother-pipes that nursed me? Now that I've felt the light, I don't think I can return to the dark."

"I will not cast you aside," Father Milagro had promised.

Yet, waiting for his eyedrops, the priest wondered how much of a requirement it was to keep promises to a creature like Ponzu. It wasn't even Ponzu, per say. The good book said all things treading the earth were made by God and all of them were good… But did that mean even sewage monsters brought to life by the unholy union of seminal fluid and what Milagro could only theorize was toxic waste?

Besides, Ponzu was a complication. A giant one.

Unlike people, sewage monsters had few reservations and fewer scruples about what was proper. If Ponzu became public knowledge, it was doubtful Ponzu would remain silent— or even vague—when asked, "So, where'd you come from?"

Ponzu wouldn't think he needed to protect Father Milagro's reputation. No, he'd probably perk up and tell everyone Father Milagro had ejaculated into a handkerchief gifted to him by his mother and, after flushing it, Ponzu was born. Ponzu, no doubt, would conjure the stained rag from within himself to show off. The jokes would soon follow. It was one thing for everyone to speculate about how the celibate endured celibacy, sure, but when there was a living, breathing reminder of it, it was different.

And there was no way to hide it. Word would spread about a living puddle of sewage and then the 24-hour news cycle would find Ponzu. He'd be interviewed and each time pull that handkerchief out for everyone to see—tv audiences, top scientists, politicians—and explain how Milagro made him.

The thought of being a punchline on late-night tv for a year made Milagro pinch the bridge of his nose, aggravating his pink eye enough to drip on his fingers.

The pharmacist called Father Milagro up and exclaimed, "Good lord, man! *That's* one helluva case of pink eye." When Father Milagro tried to hand him the prescription slip, the pharmacist refused to touch it. "Don't worry, I know what you need."

He disappeared and returned a few minutes later. While he'd been among the shelves, the pharmacist put on a surgeon's mask and two sets of latex gloves. He placed a heavy dropper-topped bottle on the counter. "Two drops, three times a day. Be careful. This stuff'll stain your cheeks. And, hey, don't give up on yourself."

Confused, Father Milagro asked, "What?"

The pharmacist pointed at the priest's eyes and whistled. "That's a real bad case. It might give these drops a scuffle, but keep at it. Those things *work*. Last time I prescribed them, it was to one of those fetish people, you know big guy in a rubber suit, that kind of thing. Father, he used to swim in septic tanks. Just rub-a-dub-dub in poop. Doctors said he'd go blind... but nope." He tapped the bottle. "These drops. They work better than bleach. Now, if we could just get him to stop with the shit-diving, am I right? Like I said, don't give up on yourself. You'll beat this yet."

The pharmacist told Milagro to have a blessed day, but Father Milagro didn't return the sentiment. A whole host of ideas had come over Father Milagro, ideas that would solve all his problems or, at least, all the ones involving Ponzu.

V.

It was luck that everyone his congregants told about the talking sewage already thought they were crazy for asking God for things in an age of science, so they took it all as gobbledygook.

It was even luckier that, in exchange for a deacon's position and a lead altar boy job for the local printer's son, Milagro got a stack of pamphlets printed overnight. Father Milagro spent a week hunting down his congregants—at work, at home—to deliver them.

The pamphlets did their best to explain what happened at the church that day. A demon, the pamphlets read, had tried to attack the church. It had been captured by Father Milagro, but he wasn't strong enough to exorcise the evil alone. He needed their help. All they had to do was go to church on Sunday (as usual) and pray as loud as they could. There was a stipulation, though. They had to—had to, had to, *had to*!—wear hunting-grade earplugs for the entirety of the mass. The sewer demon, the pamphlet explained, was like all of the devil's minions and could enchant them with lies.

While it did perturb Milagro how easily his congregants embraced his explanations, his main worry was Ponzu, who'd spent most of the week stinking up his complex and absorbing various items throughout Father Milagro's home.

At first it had just been garbage, but now Ponzu wanted to absorb sentimental things like bottle caps from shared sodas and teaspoons from their first cup of tea.

In its own way, Ponzu's affections for Milagro led to a fascination with the bible, which made it all the easier to convince Ponzu to go to the church. He worried Ponzu would see through his offer and guess at some ulterior design when Father Milagro brought up the idea of a baptism. In their week together, Father Milagro found his creation to be sharp, caring, kind, yet Ponzu seized on the idea and was giddy.

There were times, especially during his vespers, when Ponzu's naivete weighed on Milagro but then the fantasies gave him strength. The fantasy that strengthened him the night before Ponzu's baptism was horrible.

Milagro imagined himself at the altar, eucharist overhead, and Ponzu in the front row. Ponzu's scum-arms were merged in prayer and light from a stained-glass window glinted across Ponzu's liquid shape, painting his nucleus in reds and greens and purples. As the words were spoken and the grace of God flowed through Father Milagro and made the bread flesh, his gaze flowed over his parishioners onto two back-row teenagers. They pointed at Ponzu and pumped their fists over their laps, laughing, and the pandemic of laughter spread until the entire church was uproarious. Ponzu alone remained in prayer.

The day of the baptism, Milagro's daydreamed horror neutered Ponzu's devotion. It didn't matter how excited Ponzu was at the prospect of being brought into a heavenly family or that it made Ponzu ripple in joy. It didn't even matter that, when Ponzu had been left in the rectory bathroom before the baptism began, it stopped Father Milagro, saying, "I know I am a mistake—please, don't agree nor disagree. It's meaningless now, really. I just wanted to say this time with you... I'll cherish it... and I... I love you and thank you... Dad."

Father Milagro didn't flinch, reflexively saying, "And I love you... my son," as he closed the bathroom door.

Afterward, Milagro was in a dead sprint.

First, the priest ran into the church and made sure Luanne, the organist, knew the signal and wore her earplugs. Next, he opened the doors since he had to buy a family-sized inflatable pool and filled it with a mix of bleach and disinfectants. Father Milagro positioned a mop handle near the pool because he wanted to preserve the bishop's ceremonial staff. Finally, satisfied everything was in place, Father Milagro addressed his church.

Only half had shown, but there were enough to fool Ponzu. "All right, everyone," he began, pacing. "Thank you for lending me your strength. This vile, *horrible* thing has come to test our faith. But what happens today *has* to happen. This thing must be cleansed—"

"Bleach'll really hurt devil stuff?" a congregant asked.

Father Milagro paused, coughed, and continued. "Yes, um, bleach has many holy properties when mixed with holy water and... other things," he explained. "But, before we begin, let me warn you. This monster is clever. It will plead, it will cry, anything to slither into your hearts where it can make your soul stink as much as it does. So, once we begin, do not—I repeat, DO NOT—remove your earplugs. The instant you do, we'll be lost. Just keep praying. Understand? Your prayers will weaken it."

The people nodded.

"All right," he said, taking a deep, steadying breath. "Let's flush us a devil!"

"Amen," they replied, putting their earplugs in one by one.

Milagro signaled for the prayers and the music to begin.

VI.

Father Milagro had envisioned Ponzu's reaction to the pomp and ritual that accompanied catholic rites. Surely a nucleic organism of sewage bound by a telekinesis of some kind would be mesmerized by the experience. Milagro wore his special robes—a set his mother had sewn with purple flowers and chalices—and the church was filled with a cacophony of "Our Fathers" spoken offbeat from one another to the tune of Luanne hammering away at the organ. The ceremony was rendered magical by the morning-lit stained glass windows.

Yet, Ponzu rode a swell of filth toward the pool as if it was the gallows. It said nothing. Father Milagro sensed no suspicion. To him, the heavy smell of bleach was almost overpowering, but Ponzu bobbed up to the pool and considered it as Milagro opened a small prayer book.

To those watching whose ears were filled by their own frantic praying, Father Milagro truly grappled with an agent of Hell. He prayed quickly, his lips moving at nearly a blur. In one hand, he had a small bottle of holy water which he held up to Heaven or flicked at the toilet flush come to life. But the demon was strong and resisted all the priest's orders to cleanse itself in the pool.

However, had they removed their earplugs, the parishioners would've been confused. Everything they'd been told was about casting out demons and kicking devil ass, but the words didn't have any of that.

"Please accept this child into your kingdom, o Heavenly Father," Milagro said. The drizzled holy water was absorbed into Ponzu. "With these... waters wash away the original sin of Adam and Eve, the sin that was upon Ponzu since birth. Please, Heavenly Father of divine love and forgiveness, through these waters, cleanse your child, Ponzu, so he may be clean, body and soul."

Seeing the church praying hard and Luanne playing like a woman in need of a psych-eval, Father Milagro concluded.

"Now, my son, step... uh... Get into this baptismal pool to complete your first step into the loving arms of the Holy Trinity," Father Milagro went on, motioning to the pool. He put his prayer book away and took up the mop handle. "Go on, Ponzu. Everything's all right."

Ponzu's nucleus regarded him. "Are you sure, Father?"

Milagro nodded, saying, "Find strength through God, son."

Ponzu faced the pool and a ripple ran through its form, shrinking it down a little, before the living sewage willed itself into it.

The reaction was instantaneous. The living sewage bubbled on contact with the pool. As Ponzu stood among it, the water roiled. Ponzu sank deeper into the pool without a fight.

Again, he regarded his father.

Father Milagro put on a paternal grin. "Son, you must completely submerge yourself to be truly cleansed."

"But... it hurts," Ponzu warbled.

"Yes, my son, that's God purifying you so you may join his kingdom," the priest replied.

After a moment, Ponzu lifted himself as high as he could, thinning his liquid body until it swayed like a skinny tree keeping its nucleus aloft. The light played prismatic upon the little ripples of his sewage-flesh. Looking at the priest once more, Ponzu spoke. "Dad," he said. "I know."

Father Milagro didn't understand.

"I heard you through the pipes," Ponzu said, the bleach eating his body. "I thought after our time together it couldn't be true—it was a ploy, I hoped, for them"—Ponzu swept a tendril at the parishioners, painting a line of gunk across them—"Yet, here I am and there you are. Goodbye, Dad. Know that you made me and destroyed me and that will never be washed off your soul."

Ponzu willed its body around the nucleus, so it hung in the air an instant before cannonballing into the pool. The bleach splashed over the sides, soaking the carpets and the priest's robes. Milagro felt Ponzu's attention in those turbulent waters.

He wasn't sure if the cannonballing was a childish stunt of self-harm to prod Milagro into fishing Ponzu out of the pool, but whatever it was, the priest jabbed the mop handle into Ponzu's nucleus, pinning his creation down.

The priest held Ponzu there as two weak splashes of muck moved up the mop handle like terminal caterpillars. Halfway up, they died and dripped to join the rest of the filthy pool.

VII.

The pool stilled and Milagro motioned for everyone to stop praying and remove their earplugs. They did. The priest stirred the pool, now a mix of inert shit and junk—a salt shaker shaped like a bird, old bottle caps, one of Milagro's coffee mugs, the rosary Ponzu learned to pray with. The congregants didn't see a handkerchief, one that bore their priest's name, cling to the mop handle nor did they notice Milagro spear it to the bottom of the pool.

The faithful woke from their prayer-fog when Father Milagro declared, "Fear no more, my flock, the Lord has protected thee. Praise be the Lord."

They rejoiced, "Praise be the Lord."

—ETC.—

RECIPE FOR REVENGE

I.

Getting the unbaptized baby wasn't even the hardest part of Guzman's plot. That had actually been pretty simple. Guzman found some smuggler leading mojados through his fifty acres and paid the man two old guns and a cheap bottle of tequila. Afterward, the smuggler snatched an infant from a woman's arms and punched her bloody when she fought back before he gave it to Guzman.

The hardest part had been the wolf's bane. For that, Guzman had to drive into Dodd and order a mess of it from Mayela's Nursery. The flowers took three weeks to arrive and were so expensive that Guzman had to eat stale tortillas and cans of beans for weeks. He hated his plain meals but knew they'd be worth the inconvenience.

The whole idea came from a curandera who drank at the bar down the road. Over drinks, she'd told him of the skinwalkers, of the shapeshifters of old, and of their ancient recipes for acquiring such magic. The rituals, the ingredients, the words, Guzman kept the drinks flowing to get them all. She couldn't've known Guzman wasn't flirting but instead scheming for revenge.

For years, Guzman's neighbors had lodged complaints against him. Guzman's ranch was nestled in the center of four bigger plots. His acreage was full of garbage. He shot deer out of season, cut their fences, tossed bottles onto their property, and grew ratty weed. Because of Ms. Cooper of the Triple C, Mr. Boykin of Boykin Ranch, the Terrazas of Santa Cleotilde, and especially Hank Dobkin the foreman for the Lazy F Cattle Company, Guzman owed thousands in fines and had spent, off and on, months in jail.

He'd wanted to march up to their front doors, knock, and shoot his neighbors the instant they opened up. But spiteful as he was, Guzman wasn't stupid.

He knew if he killed one—or all—of his neighbors, the sheriff would pick him up within a day. Guzman had threatened them, harassed them, and it was all on the record. Until he talked with that curandera, Guzman thought he'd have to resign himself to wishing inoperable cancer on his neighbors.

But, with the baby, the wolf's bane, and a wolf skin from the taxidermist, the time was almost upon him because he wouldn't shoot his neighbors or stab them or beat them to death. Those things could come back to him. But, with his shape-shifting recipe, his neighbors would die screaming all the same and all the sheriffs in all the world would look at the grisly scenes and conclude no man did it. The only thing that could tear people open like that was a bear or cougar or—in Guzman's case—a wolf.

II.

On the full moon, Guzman took his ingredients out to a secluded spot on his ranch. He combined the ingredients as the curandera instructed.

First, he split the baby open and skinned it. The baby was weak from hunger and fought him as much as a dead jackrabbit. Guzman shaved the fat off the skin into a bucket of purple wolf's bane. He used a heavy stick to mash the mixture into a thick paste. By midnight, it was the correct consistency. Guzman spread the wolf skin on the ground and undressed in the light of the full moon.

Naked, Guzman spread handfuls of the purple muck evenly across the inner lining of the wolf skin. With each pass, Guzman felt dark energy surging through his fingers, a tantalizing feeling that filled his mind with visions of terrified neighbors.

When the entire skin was stained with the mix of wolf's bane and infant fat, Guzman picked up the fur by the forelegs and hung it on the low branches of a tree. He went back to the bucket and, squatting beside it, slathered handfuls of purple muck on his arms and legs and shoulders, even his face.

Guzman retrieved the skin and lifted it over his head. He looked at the full moon and trembled with anticipation. Once he lowered the skin across his back, the ancient magic would grant him the power to change from man to beast and back again. He would be monstrous, undying.

Already, his mind was a tempest, swirling with ideas of immortality, of the centuries of solitude and retribution on all the generations of neighbors yet unborn.

Lowering the skin, Guzman spoke. The curandera told him the actual words had little meaning, that the truest part of the bargain with the old gods was the bargainer's intent and the life destroyed.

"I make this bargain," Guzman called to the moon. "Make fur of my flesh, make moonlight of my eyes, fangs of my teeth, and claws of my fingers so I can have my revenge."

The wind swirled. Overhead, an owl flew. Guzman thought them signs and covered himself in his new flesh.

III.

Guzman lost himself to the power of the unholy ritual once the wolf skin was fully upon him. The aches and pains of his sixty hard years were gone and all that was left was a feeling of invincibility. His muscles thrummed with vigor, his bones quieted, and even the dark seemed brighter. He looked at his hands and saw claws there. His tongue ran across a mouthful of fangs sharp enough to make even the old gods bleed.

Guzman howled at the moon and ran through the brush like something born in perfect unity with the monte. He loped through the tall grass, unafraid of the rattlers or the spiders, and tore through the trees uncaring of the thorns snagging his flesh. His whole body was numb with power, numb with bloodlust.

He found the fence line separating him from the Lazy F Cattle Company. Guzman scaled it as easily as he would a gentle staircase and swung himself over the barbed wire without caution.

On the ground once more, Guzman scanned the landscape and saw Hank Dobkin's house in the distance. He cut through an empty pasture and another occupied by over three hundred head of slumbering cattle.

Passing the dozing cows, Guzman clawed at their necks and their bellies. They woke, startled, mooing wildly before running off, too dumb to know they were dying. Snarling, he tore at them with powerful claws until Guzman was sure he'd killed so many not only would Hank Dobkin die but the whole Lazy F Cattle Company as well.

Guzman felt the wolf trying to take over his senses. It tempted him to chase the cows, to leap on their backs and bite their necks, and Guzman almost did until a rifle shot pierced the sounds of his slaughter.

In a fury, Guzman saw Dobkin standing in his open doorway, rifle pointed in the air. The sight of Dobkin doubled Guzman over. His fangs gnashed and his claws wriggled because Dobkin would be the first of many and the popgun in his hands would only get the man killed quicker. There would be blood. So much blood.

IV.

It was birthing season so when the cattle started making noise, Hank Dobkin wasn't surprised. It was probably a pack of coyotes sniffing around for a stray calf. Though he doubted the little canines could get past the mother cows—hormonal and half a ton a piece—Hank got his .270 anyway. He didn't bother to put clothes on.

He'd heard the bovine ruckus and popped the safety off. Dobkin didn't fire straight up, instead shooting off in the direction of Guzman's place, thinking it wouldn't be so bad if he hit the mean son of a bitch by accident. Dobkin expected to hear a few nervous yips after the shot and, within a minute or two, the herd would quiet down and he could get some sleep for tomorrow's work.

What came out of the dark startled him.

Ed Guzman was like Dobkin had never seen him. Sure, Guzman often wandered drunk, clad only in an undershirt, briefs, and a pair of boots on his property, but now the man was basically nude except for the animal skin across his shoulders and the purple muck smeared across his flabby body.

Strange as it all was, the look in Guzman's eyes put Dobkin back a step. Those eyes were wide and intense and sank into Dobkin with a murderous intent.

Guzman clawed at the air between them. He was talking half-formed words mixed with throaty growls and he snapped his jaws at Hank with each step.

"What the fuck you doing, Goozmin?" Hank asked.

Though he was still yards away, Guzman raked his fingers at Dobkin to scare him.

"Get back to your side of the fence before I get the sheriff," Hank said, gripping the rifle in both hands. "I won't tell you twice."

Guzman barked at him.

Hank leveled his rifle. "Get the fuck on or so help me..."

Guzman stared at the rifle barrel and, for a second, Hank thought that would be the end of it. Guzman would leave and they'd return to giving each other dirty looks through the fence. But Guzman laughed like a man possessed. Another series of guttural sounds came from his mouth and Guzman leaped, clawed fingers outstretched.

Hank pulled the trigger.

The rifle was made to stop tougher things than men. The bullet caught Guzman a few inches beneath the collarbone and sent him into a half somersault. He landed face down in the dirt.

Hank kept the rifle aimed at Guzman until some of the other cattlemen, some armed themselves, came out to see what had happened.

They looked from Guzman—naked legs splayed out and dyed ass in the air—to Hank, who lowered his rifle by degrees.

"What happened?" one of them asked.

Hank leaned his rifle against the doorframe and shook his head. "Call the sheriff. Tell him Ed Goozmin finally lost his goddamn mind."

—ETC.—

ACKNOWLEDGMENTS

"Thin Soup" was originally published in *Chilling Tales for Dark Nights* (**s5 ep16**).

"The Voice in Your Guts" was originally published in *Sanitarium, no. 2.*

"Devotion to the Dead" was originally published in *Chilling Tales for Dark Nights* (**s5 ep16**).

"The First Cup" was originally published in *Road Kill: Texas Horror by Texas Writers, Volume 5.*

"Grand Electric Gestures of Love" was originally published in *Ink Stains v. 9.*

"A Whistle in the Dark" was originally published in *Road Kill: Texas Horror by Texas Writers v. 2.*

"The Chickens That Are Not Their Chickens" was originally published in *Road Kill: Texas Horror by Texas Writers, Volume 6.*

"Leonard and the Carousel" was originally published in *Deadman's Tome eZine.*

"WE SELL PICKLES" was originally published in *Chilling Tales for Dark Nights* (**s1 ep28**).

"Recipe for Revenge" was originally published in *Chilling Tales for Dark Nights* (**s5 ep16**).

ABOUT THE ARTIST

Jorge Javier Lopez is an artist from Texas. He was born and resides on the border. He has exhibited his paintings and drawings in galleries and museums for over 20 years.

About the Author

Mario E. Martinez is the author of *San Casimiro, Texas: Short Stories*, *A Pig Named Orrenius & Other Strange Tales*, *Ashtree*, *NEO-Laredo*, and *The Glowing Pigs of El Cenizo*. He lives somewhere in South Texas. His works are available at marioemartinez.squarespace.com